Water

Water

Sue Thomas

Five Leaves Publications

For my daughters Amber and Erin

Water
by Sue Thomas

Published in 1995 by Five Leaves Publications
PO Box 81, Nottingham NG5 4ER

0 907123511

Printed in Great Britain by Antony Rowe
© Sue Thomas 1994
Cover painting by Sue Sareen

Part One

Orford, Suffolk, A.D. 1197

...certain Fishers of the sea tooke in their Nettes a Fish having the shape of a man in all pointes, which Fish was kept by Bartlemew de Glanville, Custos of the Castle of Orforde in the same Castle by the same space of six monethes, and more for a wonder.

He spake not a word.

All manner of meates he gladly did eat, but more greedilie raw fish after he had crushed out all the moisture.

Oftentimes he was brought to the church where he showed no tokens of adoration.

At length when he was not well looked to, he stale away to the sea and never after appeared.

Ralph of Coggeshall

Most murders, like most accidents, happen at home, but Julie's father hadn't actually been home for many years so she never got the opportunity to stab him in the kitchen. Neither could she throw an electric fire into his bath, or trip him up at the top of the stairs.

In the end she was forced to take her chances on the open ocean and there, just off the coast of Scotland, she drowned him because she thought he deserved it.

He probably did.

We've all been damaged by our parents, God knows, but few of us have the guts to do anything about it.

Sometimes it's a mother who's too possessive — or maybe not possessive enough. Sometimes it's a father who comes and goes — or goes and never comes back. That's what Simon did, although in fairness to him he certainly wasn't the first. Read the statistics. Most kids end up with their Mums, and by the end of three years most divorced Dads have disappeared. It's a fact, and there's no denying it.

We're supposed to feel sorry for these men because they're simply not equipped to deal with their emotions.

Tough.

It's about time they learned then, isn't it?

Of course, there are always plenty more fish in the sea — but do any of them make a better catch?

The male Deep Sea Angler fish, for instance, has a parasitic lifestyle not unlike that of many husbands of our acquaintance. When he finds a female Deep Sea Angler fish the first thing he does is bite onto the side of her body. (He is tiny, she is HUGE.) He clings on for grim death until their flesh gradually fuses together and they are as one.

Just like in marriage.

Of course he can't use his mouth for eating any more but that's okay, because he's hooked into her system and she'll feed him from her own body for the rest of his life. And, like any loving couple, they can have babies. He just wiggles his tiny bum and fertilises her eggs from where he is.

In their case, of course, there certainly *aren't* plenty of other fish in the sea because they can't get away from each other.

Ever.

It's for life, God help them.

And then there's the Great White Shark, which doesn't bother killing its prey but simply rips large chunks out of its still-living victim, only leaving the poor thing alone when it's full to bursting. Burp! Pardon me.

There are men like that, too.

After Simon swam away to join the swelling shoal of migrating husbands, Julie watched her mother as she painfully struggled to make a new life. The child was an onlooker to various fumbling love-affairs, outbursts of guilt and anger, and crazy spending sprees followed by anxiety when the bills came in. Although she was only very small when Simon left, she never forgot the hours she spent huddling under the bed-covers while Ruth cried on the phone to various friends or raced around the house smashing happy-family photos.

Most children blame themselves when their parents split up, but Julie didn't see it that way. For her it was crystal clear. First Ruth was happy, and then she wasn't. The dividing line was Simon's departure, and it was as simple as that. True, during the years that followed Ruth was not always the best of parents — but then, who is? On the whole Julie was certain that everything would have been okay again if Simon would only come back, and the fact that he didn't put the blame squarely in his court. (Nevertheless, it was not when Simon left, but when Ruth found her dream lover that the little family really started to fall apart.)

Julie hadn't always planned to kill her father. But when the opportunity finally came it was just too good to resist, and so she acted on behalf of all those single-parent children around the world who still wonder why Daddy never phones.

Our story starts not with Simon's departure, nor with his watery demise, but at the time in between. It was then that Julie, fourteen years old and never-been-kissed, began to learn about men and what they do.

When Julie was fourteen, she and her mother built an ornamental pond in their back garden.

A flat square of still water, it ran down below the surface to more than two feet deep in parts. Beyond its fibreglass walls lay a hostile stratum of clay and stones, just beneath the topsoil and too barren for cultivation, whilst within the safe confines of the pool preformed shelves and crannies gave the few goldfish a truly subterranean environment.

Digging it had been back-breaking work, but mother and

daughter had laboured together through the month of October, taking turns to chip with a spade through the glutinous clay.

It was necessary to fit the shape of the hole exactly to the preformed walls. Ruth built up one surface then scraped down another whilst Julie lowered the body of the pond at different angles, using a plank and a long spirit-level to keep the top straight.

At last it fitted.

In celebration, Ruth threw a weary arm around her daughter's shoulders and hugged her. They could feel pleased with themselves although now, after a long day working in the mud, the dark Autumn night was drawing in fast. Determined to finish, they dragged a bag of sand from the boot of the car and sprinkled it hastily over the smooth planes of the hole, then fitted in the pond, shuffling it slightly until it came to rest. Julie fetched the garden hose and they began to fill the fibreglass slowly, keeping a close eye on the shifting levels.

Standing arm-in-arm, leaning against each other with fatigue, they silently watched the water lap against the grey interior walls of the pond. Their spines were sore from bending, boots thick with mud, hands grimy and lacerated by the gritty sub-soil. The water churned and bubbled, climbed slowly until it reached the rim, then suddenly began to spill with abandon onto the surrounding paving. Ruth ran to turn off the hose as plant debris and leaves swirled chaotically on the surface of the pool.

A glowing moon had arisen to flash its brightening light across the caged and turbulent water as it strove to escape the confines of the fibreglass enclosure, and in appeasement its captors quickly fed the pool with lilies in weighted pots, pond irises, and oxygenating weed. It gulped down the plants one by one, closing over them like a liquid trap-door, until gradually the surface slowly began to compose itself.

The next day, after the water had settled, Ruth and Julie gently lowered in a polythene bag containing six plump goldfish. Immediately the bag ballooned and flipped about in the ripples as if at any moment it would toss the fish straight into the chilly water. Ruth steadied it, jamming it against the side with stones, and left it for an hour until the temperatures inside and outside had equalised.

After tea, Julie, for this was to be her honour, gently tipped the bag, making sure there were no goldfish trapped in the corners, until the six swam out and down to the cloudy depths, where they would hardly be seen again for the next few months.

Freshwater habitats are highly subject to changes in water levels.

As the water level falls the fish population may become separated, and since freshwater lakes provide such varied habitats it's very likely that each fish-community will begin to evolve differently from its former family.

Even if, in the future, the water levels rise again and bring them back together they will probably have already evolved into new and different species and will no longer be capable of interbreeding.

Ruth was making vegetable soup on the evening when her daughter climbed into the car of a total stranger and was whisked off to a country lay-by.

Preparing a good soup is an act of meditation. A sharp knife, a cutting board, and a gardenful of vegetables.

First she put a heavy pan to warm over a gentle heat. Then as the oil began to spread she started to wash and chop.

Meanwhile, he put his arm around Julie's neck and pulled her towards him until their mouths touched. His cheeks were smooth and his lips wet.

She didn't know what to do.

The last time a man had touched her she was three years old and it was her father giving her a chaste kiss on the chin. Of that memory, only the mixed odours of after-shave and whisky remained. She didn't really know anything about men, except that they had lots of ways to hurt you and you had to be careful.

One thing she did know was that you should open your mouth to kiss but at this moment her whole sense of decency rebelled and she kept her lips tightly closed as he pushed against her.

'Open up, darling,' he murmured, and at the same time he put his hand inside her blouse and felt around her small breasts until his fingers located a nipple.

She froze.

The car stank of beer and tobacco and a broken spring dug into her back as he crushed against her flesh.

She tried to breathe shallowly through her nose while her lips went numb under the pressure of his teeth.

4

Onions are fearsome in their resistance.

Like cornered insects they sprayed their stinging chemicals into Ruth's face as she peeled away their skins piece by piece, all the while squinting through tear-filled eyes at the process of the blade. Then she paused for a moment to wipe the back of her wrist across her cheeks.

As her mother wept onions, Julie's eyes too filled up with tears, but she would not be able to speak until she had pushed him away from her mouth. She struggled beneath him, and he thought she was enjoying it.

He'd been so nice earlier on, when she and Dawn chatted up him and his friend outside the shops.

'Want to come for a drive?' he'd said.

'Why not?' She'd smiled up at him with tight lips so he wouldn't see her crooked front tooth. He was freshly-shaven, straight out of the bath, and ready for a good night out.

'Like a fag?'

'I don't smoke, thanks.'

The habit disgusted her, but at the same time she felt thrilled that this was the first time in her life she had been offered a cigarette.

As he cupped his hands to light up she noticed there was a fine line of black along his nails, and that his knuckles were cut and calloused.

'What about your friend?' he said.

'Oh, she won't mind. I'll see her tomorrow at...' she hesitated '...at work.'

Dawn was leaning heavily against the shop-window, deep in conversation. As she talked, she kicked one foot against the other and laughed a lot.

He called to his friend and they regrouped — the young men a couple of doors away, Dawn and Julie next to the Post Office.

'Guess what? He's got a car!' exclaimed Julie triumphantly. 'Has yours?'

'He hasn't said.' replied Dawn, rather disgruntled. Then she brightened up. 'I'm not bothered anyway. He's alright. Is my make-up OK?'

'Yeah. You look great. Hey, shut up, they're coming back.'

It was then that Julie realised something.

'If he's got a car,' she mused, 'he must be at least seventeen...'

They grinned at each other, and Dawn winked.

'See you! Don't do anything I wouldn't do!'

As they drove away Julie turned to wave, but the other couple had already disappeared into the shadows.

A continental aroma rose from the olive oil, making Ruth remember cool spanish salad. She recalled slices of onion and tomatoes as big as grapefruits, and bread to absorb the oily juice with rough wine to soak up the sun.

Into this pool of Mediterranean memories she slid her belligerent English onions. They hissed against the soothing murmur of the oil for a second, then submitted and began to soften. Ruth slammed on the lid triumphantly and left them to sweat it out. Fair reward for hurting her eyes so much. She rinsed her hands under the tap.

Garlic put up less opposition, and in it went with the subdued onions.

So far so good. Ruth wiped her knife.

'Stop it!' Julie pushed him away.

'What's the matter?'

His lips were puffy red and his face the breathless white of a drowned man. His air of distraction frightened her for a moment, then he gathered himself and forced a smile.

'I just want you to stop.' she repeated.

She picked up her shoulder bag and opened the door. Outside, the November air felt like dark smoke on her skin, and she wondered which direction to start walking. Then he was out of the car too, his cigarette lighter flaming up in front of her. On the grass beside the kerb she could see a lorry tyre blown to ribbons of steel and rubber.

As with humans, most types of fish are born either male or female, and stay that way, but some species have developed more interesting alternatives:-

Hermaphrodites
One individual is both sexes, and able to breed independently.

Synchronous Hermaphrodites
Some fish — bass, for example — are able to be both sexes at the same time, and reproduce by exchanging eggs and spawn.

Successive Hermaphrodites
These species begin life as one sex then change to the other as they mature. For example, wrasse live in harem communities controlled by a dominant male — but this male will have begun life as a female.

Individuals which begin life as a male and later change to female tend only to occur in species which do not hold territories, like many deep-sea species, or in species like the anemone fish where the territory is controlled by the female.

Some species, instead of being hermaphrodites, have different kinds of males.

The Atlantic Salmon has two types. Males which have returned from the sea are big with an upturned jaw sporting teeth developed for fighting, whereas those which have not yet been to sea are too small to fight a big male successfully or to court a female — but they can sneak into the nest and fertilize some of the eggs.

The North American Freshwater Sunfish has three:-

1) Large males, able to court females and build nests.

2) Small sneaker males, who creep into the nest unnoticed.

3) Female impersonators whose unthreatening appearance ensures that they are tolerated in the nest.

To reproduce, most female fish shed their eggs into the water whilst the male adds his sperm. The eggs must be fertilised almost immediately or both they and the sperm will die. A few viviparous species give birth to live young, whilst other species retain the eggs within the fish's body until they hatch.

Ruth turned on the radio and Albinoni danced into the kitchen. Next to the chopping board she set a few potatoes, some carrots, leeks and a jar of orange lentils. What else would she need? Humming along with the music, she opened the fridge. There were plenty more vegetables, but to make a good soup you must exercise self-control. She considered adding a piece of limp celery, but cooked celery tends towards too much sweetness. And cauliflower goes soggy if you're not careful. Fresh spinach? She licked her lips at the thought, but it was too late in the season and there was none left in the garden. Parsnips? Too sweet again. Peas, beans, sweet-corn, mushrooms... no. Keep it simple.

Instead she would cut some parsley. She took up her torch and her deadly knife and went outside leaving the back-door open. Albinoni tripped lightly behind.

It was so fresh, so invigorating, to be out in the dark. The scent of last week's bonfire still hung in the air and she breathed it in deeply.

It was so good sometimes, just to feel yourself alive.

Julie didn't know what to do. One minute he was all over her pawing and groping, then the next he seemed quite nice. Just now he was sitting on the bonnet of the car and pointing out the night stars.

'There's the Plough. Look, over there.' He took a drag of his cigarette and turned to her grinning with nerves.

'I'm not that bad, am I?'

No, no he wasn't so bad at all, as long as he kept his distance. She felt very foolish. She thought of the number of times she'd wondered what it was like to be kissed, and yet now she was revolted by it all.

She'd never tasted someone else's spit before. And no-one had ever caressed those small breasts she had grown. She hadn't allowed even her mother to see them, and yet now this person without a name had reached into her blouse and touched her without asking.

'Can you take me home now please?'

He was losing her. 'Are you sure? It's only just after eight. I though we could go for a drink...'

'I can't. I've got to see my cousin. She's coming round at nine. I've got to go.'

He didn't believe that, but he also realised the evening wasn't going to work out, and he was embarrassed at the way he'd jumped on her. Girls never seemed to like the way he kissed. He wondered how Gary was getting on with her friend.

He flicked his cigarette into the bushes and smiled uncomfortably.

'Come on then. I'll take you back.'

When Julie entered the house she smelled the wonderful aroma of home. Ruth was cutting bread in the kitchen.

'You're on time!' she called out cheerfully. 'Supper's nearly ready.'

Julie went upstairs and scrubbed at her teeth, spitting vigorously until every trace of the taste of him was washed from her mouth.

She felt sure that Ruth would notice a change, but she was wrong. On that occasion anyway. Her mother never knew what had happened that night, but Julie told Dawn all about it at school the next day. Well, she told her a version of it, and Dawn related a similar one in return. So how do you ever find out the truth?

But as time went by the episode seemed to take on the golden glow of romance, and Julie determined she would be better next time. After all, she told herself, she had only just turned fifteen, and she had to start somewhere.

During the first week of December the sky bloomed heavily with continual fog. A sharp sun gaped through the regular sweep of pale grey like the disc of light left by a hot coin against a frosted window.

The new pond was soon frozen, a thick layer of ice gluing it together from edge to edge.

Each morning Julie boiled up a kettle and tiptoed outside in her thin dressing-gown to pour the steaming water evenly across the surface of the pool.

The sunken fish were preying on her mind.

Since the freeze began she had suffered every night from dark dreams where she was trapped in the depths of the pond, soundless and mute beneath the crusted ice. Through the clouded surface above she could just make out the face of her mother calling, her mouth opening and closing. But no voice penetrated the frozen glass of Julie's fishworld. When, in her dream, Julie wept, every tear only increased the volume of water above her head and pushed Ruth's desperate calls even further away.

So, upon waking, she immediately went downstairs to boil her kettles. Often she would find her mother already there, and together they would peer worriedly into the soupy ice until the hot water had melted a small hole. Then with a sharp crack the rim of the pool would relax, and they prodded it, trying to ease it further open with fingers chilling until they burned, in the hope that fresh oxygen would filter down to the shrouded creatures below and keep them alive.

But when they returned home in the fast-falling winter dusk the hole would be frozen over again. The pond was busy. During the day it would melt a little, evaporate a little, then freeze again. Each time it would sweat warmth into the garden air so that invisibly, and with apparent contradiction, the faster it froze the more heat it sent into the shimmering ether.

Despite this small contribution there was still no sign of a thaw. Although the pond was caught in the sunlight and forced to labour through constant change, other parts of the garden received no relief during the day and by nightfall more frost would have formed over the previous layers. And some plants chilled faster than others. The thick-leaved mexican orange had only a dusting of ice around the leaf-edges, but the sprawling snow-in-summer became snow-in-winter too, its delicate grey foliage heavily encrusted with granules of hard frost.

Some days, in their battle against fish suffocation, they would carefully break slices of ice from the surface of the pond and place the shards on the paving like broken windows, crunched and clattering underfoot.

The garden hung in suspension for over a week, its tall hedges whitening into plastic Christmas trees. Empty milk-bottles stood chilled and pale on the doorstep - cocktail glasses coated with sugar. Only a left-over baby pumpkin glowed like a single amber traffic light in the sea of sharply glittering soil.

One morning Ruth called Julie to look at the spiders' webs. On the hydrangea hung a hollow silver cage, closely spun at the base then widening out towards the top to make a spherical hammock of fine lacework. And the empty washing-line was strung with necklaces of frost clustered along almost invisible threads, each wooden peg linked to the next by a strand of icy string.

10

25th of December.

The country was cold.

Although the frost had eased slightly during the past fortnight, it had never retreated enough to melt the surface of the pond, and so the six goldfish continued to slumber in its depths.

During the night, three spirits had been and gone and now a snowy Dickensian hush lay over the Northern hemisphere.

Early church bells rang out through air as clean as toothpaste, and it was a proper Christmas. A Christmas card Christmas.

Waking, Ruth immediately sensed the special atmosphere. She pushed back her quilt and ran into the next bedroom.

'Look!'

She threw open the curtains to reveal big white flakes drifting down beyond the glass and disappearing out of view. The snow was falling so heavily that you could barely see through the misted window to the woolly grey sky beyond.

Suddenly the room seemed warmer than before.

The carpet was thicker and fluffier between their bare toes, and the old-fashioned radiator positively glowed with heat.

Ruth wiped the flat of her palm across the glass and large globules of condensation ran down her fingers with a thorough wetness which surprised her.

'Come on!' cried Julie, hurriedly putting on her clothes. 'Snow pancakes!'

This was a ritual. Every year, as soon as the first snow arrived, they would dash outside with a glass bowl and a tablespoon. Four scoops of clean snow can be substituted for eggs. Try it! The pancakes don't taste any different, but you are dining on a most ephemeral ingredient...

When she was small, Julie would suck mouthfuls of snow from the spoon, her lips numbed by the freezing metal.

That morning even the opening of the presents was delayed until they had eaten their fill.

Then Ruth, as usual, gave Julie everything she'd asked for and more. She loved to see her tearing off the paper as if she were a little child again, so she wrapped each present separately to ensure that the fun lasted for as long as possible.

Walkman batteries.

Pound coin.

Fountain pen.

T-shirt.

A novel, carefully chosen.

11

Jeans.

A Walkman to put the batteries in.

Cassette tapes.

Another pound coin — no, it's a TWO pound coin.

Writing pads.

Sketch pads.

Large bottle of bubble bath.

Small bottle of perfume...

...until, half an hour later, the floor was strewn with wrappings and they were both exhausted with pleasure. But Ruth had not yet received her gift...

Julie smiled secretively, put on her coat and boots, and trudged through the snow to the garage.

She was gone for quite a while, and Ruth was beginning to worry that something terrible had happened to her mysterious present, when Julie appeared at the lounge window, rapping on the glass and beckoning her over.

At first she could see nothing beyond the heavy flakes of snow whirling around Julie's rosy cheeks. Then she realised that there was something standing by the pond.

'What is it?'

'You'll have to come outside and look!'

She did, and it was beautiful. It was magical.

She had never seen one before, never known it was possible to own one, but there by the pool crouched a merman carved in stone. He was unlike the few pictures she had seen, where the creature is depicted as bearded and sinister. This merman was clean-shaven with the smooth features of a Michelangelo. His short curls gathered around the nape of his neck and a garland of real seashells hung across his chest.

Ruth reached out and found that in that chill garden only the merman was warm to the touch. By some magic the snow could not settle on his stony frame, but melted and ran down his body in tiny rivulets to the pool below.

Julie was delighted.

'Isn't he great? As soon as I saw him I thought that's exactly what we need for the pond! Isn't he beautiful?'

Ruth was speechless.

Usually, she hated garden ornaments.

Usually she would not for one moment consider degrading her garden with such an object.

But this was not like that at all. It — he — did, in fact, look right.

He seemed to suit the place. He seemed at home.

'Julie,' she announced with a grin, 'it's the best present I've ever had. I can't tell you why, but I just know it is. Thank you!'

Indoors again, they watched the merman from the window. As the temperature of the stone from which he was made began to equalise with the outside air the snow was able to settle on his head and shoulders, and soon he was cloaked in white.

Meanwhile, Ruth searched through her shelves looking for an old and tattered poetry book, then leafed through until she came to the right page.

'I learned this by heart at school, but I've forgotten most of it now. It's by Matthew Arnold. Listen...'

> *Come, dear children, let us away;*
> *Down and away below!*
> *Now my brothers call from the bay,*
> *Now the great winds shoreward blow,*
> *Now the salt tides seaward flow;*
> *Now the wild white horses play,*
> *Champ and chafe and toss in the spray....*

'It's called *The Forsaken Merman*. His wife has deserted him to live on land, and left behind her children as well, so they have to go back to the sea without her.

> *'Sand-strewn caverns, cool and deep,*
> *Where the winds are all asleep...*

'And they live in a palace with

> *'A ceiling of amber,*
> *A pavement of pearl...*

She laid down the book to look once more out of the window at the snow-covered statue outside, and fell silent with her own sea-going thoughts.

And so another winter passed. But this time the fragile silver cage of family was melting with it as Julie prepared to step into the world.

The following summer they took their annual vacation, travelling northwards in anticipation of long empty beaches and cold sea winds.

The A1 temporarily dissolved into the Tyne and they queued an hour for the Tunnel. Then they dipped down beneath the fish and barnacled ships and the bones of Roman soldiers while the car swam in headlights to the farther bank. Gurgling into the air again they emerged on the other side and knew the sea could not be far away.

First, they visited Holy Island.

On the way the petrol-stained verges of the road turned to red, lit up with rose-bay willow-herb looking from a distance like miles of Scottish heather as they travelled through gentle rolling hills and deeper forests. Past Chillingham where the cattle are but they did not stop until they came to the causeway. Then, fearful of drowning, they drove across the salted tarmac, past the rescue towers for those caught by the tide, and on towards a series of dunes rising gently from the sea-bed.

It was August Bank Holiday, and crowds of tourists had already arrived in coaches and cars and homes-on-wheels to experience the lonely spirituality of Lindisfarne amongst the ice-cream vans and the sellers of crabmeat sandwiches. They paid their car-park fees and wandered pilgriming over the island alone with a thousand others. It was necessary to use the imagination, and with it each individual painted bleak winter shores and romantic hardship. Every visitor had this idea as they stared beyond the rows of vehicles to an earlier time when the only rewards of a visit here were physical suffering and proximity to God.

Ruth and Julie did not stay long. They were disappointed. Especially Ruth, who had hoped to see a miracle. Or at the very least, a mermaid.

Then on to Bamburgh — a stupendous stretch of beach with the castle to the north and the Farnes bubbling up to the south.

Ruth swam in the bitter sea while Julie sunbathed on sand as clean as a shroud and watched children rock-pooling nearby. They were poking sea-anemones with sticks to make them close up. In the dunes, families barbecued their sausages a few yards from lovers curled together against the wind, each group hidden from the other behind hummocks of sea-grass which cut the children's fingers and whipped dogs' eyes as they ran for rabbits.

When Ruth returned from her swim Julie went in search of a beach-side cafe, while her mother draped her wet towel across the rocks and then sat, knees drawn up under her chin, gazing eastward.

Ships voyaged up and down in the distance. She took a deep breath and leaped on board to watch the water churning above the propeller. The deck felt solid enough, but below it the vessel perched on an endless deep. Beneath that — a chilling darkness. Another world going about its watery business. Above it was the boat, and she was on the boat, standing with the spray skimmed off from the very top of that other world clinging to her clothes like jewels.

And gulls followed the slip-stream.

She was a gull, sweeping on the currents, soaring up and diving down to catch the left-overs of a seaman's dinner. Screeching and fighting for more. Resting on the wheel-house roof, hitching a ride.

In the far distance a red and white column rose from the sea-bed.

And then she was a light-house keeper, living circularly, waiting for the last big wave to put an end to it. Fishing off the rock in calm weather, casting a line down into the deeps. On lonely days walking round and round the top of the slumbering light imagining someone to talk to. Looking down at the water which never ceased its assault against the intruder.

Down below, in the ocean, she became a cod-fish navigating the darkness, immune to the cold...

...but it's too cold down there for her. She's had enough. Bring her back to the shore-line, wash her up on the beach with a rug and a packet of sandwiches. Let the day soften towards evening and the light-house begin to spin.

As the beach emptied they took a last stroll along the water's edge to find presents left by the retreating tide — a length of orange acrylic rope, the usual plastic bottle, and a large sea-urchin. Its sea-bed coloured shell was intact, but it was dead and gave off a foul smell. Julie refused to touch it, but her mother was entranced. It was a gift from the waves. She placed it carefully on a rock to dry, leaving it for future visitors.

A chilling breeze was rising from the water and making their teeth chatter, so they made for the car and drove to a landlocked hotel to buy food and warmth.

After dinner Ruth settled down in the cosy lounge-bar to read and drink whisky while Julie, in search of adventure, wandered the few streets until she discovered a wide green park with a lake.

As she sat by the water counting ducks and waiting for something to happen, he came and sat beside her. His throat was bare but for a silver St. Christopher medal. Hello, he said, w. *c*'s your name? He smiled a lot with searching eyes and his voice was Geordie soft.

They hired a rowing boat and splashed around the lake for an hour, then he bought ice-creams and they searched for a quiet spot amongst the bushes. When she had finished her ice Julie lay down and tasted his cool mouth for afters.

This was her holiday event.

He penetrated her quickly and there was little blood. As she lay beneath him she noticed that someone had thrown a bread-bag of sandwiches into a nearby lilac. It hung amongst the branches like a musty Christmas tree decoration.

Afterwards they lay together in the summer dusk and he showed her his name. It was tattooed on his upper arm though he had never been to sea. When it was time to go she kissed him goodbye and he hung his St. Christopher around her neck.

He was the third man ever to touch her. He was nicer than the boy in the car. She wondered whether her father had worn a chain round his neck, and decided that probably he had. But she really couldn't remember.

Ruth put down her book.

'You've been a long time,' she said. 'I was beginning to think you were lost.'

'No. I was exploring. And look what I found...' Julie held out the medallion for her mother to examine.

'Mmm. Don't suppose it's worth anything.'

'No.'

Ruth fumbled in her handbag.

'I've brought the cards,' she said. 'Are you ready for a game?'

Julie stood up and took her jacket, folding it to hide the grass-stains.

'I don't think I want to play tonight.'

'Alright. You're tired, aren't you? I'll come and tuck you in.'

'No, it's OK.' She fingered the St. Christopher and looked around the quiet bar at the couples engaged in murmured conversation. 'I just want to be on my own.'

Ruth raised her eyebrows. On holiday they always ended the evening with a game of cards. Always.

'OK,' she said, putting the pack away with an unsure

cheerfulness. 'See you later then.'

'Right.'

Released, Julie hurried out of the room. As her mother watched her go she noticed that the childish bounce seemed to have left her step to be replaced by an almost imperceptible swing of the hips.

Ruth's heart was suddenly chilled with loneliness at the way her daughter had spoken to her. She sounded like an acquaintance, like a passing stranger with better things to do than play cards with a middle-aged woman.

Oh, she thought, we say we look forward to them leaving home and giving us back our freedom, but in truth can we properly imagine it? Are we ever fully prepared for the day they choose other company in preference to our own?

And how does it feel to be suddenly hurled into the abyss of a solitary life when you have always had your child to depend upon?

How does it feel?

Terrible.

She bought herself another whisky and pretended to read her book until the lounge began to empty. Then she went upstairs to their room, where Julie slept soundly thumb in mouth, her teddy tucked in beside her.

They had lived alone since Julie's third birthday when Simon had come home late, drunk, and with something to say. The usual, yet still Ruth had been devastated by the surprise of it. Another woman, another job, and all planned behind her back.

She couldn't really take it in. It had never occurred to her that he might do this, and she realised how unimaginative she must have been. She should have started worrying long ago, that much was clear, but now it was far too late.

She had picked up wrapping paper and party cake crumbs from the carpet while he stood by the kitchen door and mumbled his apologies. She accepted them without a murmur or word of reproach, too busy wondering where she'd failed as a wife.

Julie was asleep when he kissed her goodbye and then he was gone.

The Story of Alex

Alex took a pleasure in uncovering things. Trained as a chef, he liked to crack eggs by inserting his thumb into the broken edges

17

and prising them open like a newly-purchased book. He peeled potatoes and apples with the sharpest of knives and used the point to cut out any brown parts and potato eyes (he preferred his vegetables blind.)

He dropped ripe tomatoes into a bowl then poured boiling water over them until their skin writhed and shrunk and he could slip it off between his fingers.

But best of all, he liked shellfish.

He liked to keep a crab for a couple of days before he cooked it. Once a day he gave it a swim in a washing-up bowl of sea-water, then he wrapped it in layers of thick sacking soaked in brine and put it in the fridge. He was always careful not to keep it too long, because a starved crab doesn't taste as good.

Alex had never agreed with the traditional method of throwing the live animal into a pan of boiling water. It takes at least a minute to die and the shell sometimes utters a distressing scream when the air is pressured out. Sometimes, too, it might even attempt to climb out of the pot or throw a claw in its agony — which limb would then have to be thrown back in again. Altogether a messy and difficult business.

Instead, he preferred to put the crab into a pan and cover it with cold salted water. He heated the water very slowly, until it reached a temperature of about 70F, by which time the creature was unconscious. At 75F it suffocated. Then he brought the pan to a rolling boil and cooked the crab to perfection. He liked this method best because the animal suffered no distress and therefore its corpse was not flooded with the poisons produced by fear. This way the meat was always excellent with plenty of the tasty moist pink curd which dries up so quickly after death.

Alex married a woman called Laura and a year later the surgeons split her open and uncovered a pair of twins. Afterwards they closed her up again but Alex no longer knew what to do with her. Pregnancy and a caesarian had left her body wider both inside and out and there were no secrets left for him to unwrap. So he returned to his kitchen and its unexplored anatomical delights, both animate and inanimate.

But he grew bored.

After several years there was nothing he did not know about the internal organs of his prey. He had explored fruits and

18

vegetables from most parts of the known agricultural world and examined the entrails of fish from the deepest oceans. He had poached, sauteed, roasted, boiled and stir-fried nearly every species of edible animal to be found in both hemispheres.

Uncovering had become mechanical and unrewarding and he began to search for other things to slice.

When the twins were almost old enough for school he took his family on a camping holiday. They set up their tent in a sloping green field and went to explore.

On the other side of the hill Alex was thrilled to discover an exposure larger than his wildest imaginings. Nearly an acre of pasture lay peeled away before his eyes. The soil was stripped of turf and sectioned like a bullock marked off for butchering, and all over its body squirmed dozens of people scraping and digging at the wound.

At first light the next morning he followed the pegs and string across the corpse, and when the team arrived at eight they found him begging to be allowed to join them. They were pleased to find that he had a delicate touch with the trowel and was not inclined to sabotage the careful mapping of the site by pulling finds haphazardly from the ground. Instead, he liked to take his time, paring away gently at the surface, slowly revealing post-holes and shards with equal care.

While her husband discovered archaeology, Laura took the twins to the town and the sea-side and the fair and every evening, after the diggers left, Alex lead his family around the site and carefully taught them everything he had himself learned that day.

On returning from holiday he did not find it difficult to get a place at the local university, and since the twins were starting school Laura was happy to take a part-time job at the corner shop. They even found that a student grant was nearer to their former income than they'd expected.

So Alex left the kitchen and went to uncover more secrets.

During his first weeks he acquired a lot of information, the most important being that every question has several answers and that nothing can ever be considered conclusive. It looked as if it was going to take him a long time to uncover even just a few things.

He also found that the students took lecture notes at break-neck speed, which dismayed him since the only thing he had written in ten years were restaurant menus. He swallowed his pride and spent his evenings copying and re-reading his scribbled sheets while Laura bathed the twins and listened to their stories of school.

19

And he found that the seminar room had a quite unexpectedly informal atmosphere. He was surprised to learn that even though his tutor was called Dr Murdoch, she introduced herself as Ruth. It was difficult to get used to, especially since she seemed to be already in possession of a great deal of the knowledge he was working so hard to acquire and he felt awed in her presence.

In the first week Alex struggled hard to keep up with the torrent of information flowing from the lectern. Chastened and nervous, he attended Ruth's seminar that afternoon with a feeling of dread. He was sure to be exposed as an ignorant kitchen-worker with no business in this institute of higher learning.

However, once closeted in the stuffy room with a dozen other students he realised she was only a woman, and a poorly dressed one at that. Immediately his sense of threat disappeared. She wore no make-up but her lips were full and red, and her waist was thickened like Laura's, with the slightly dropped buttocks of motherhood. Laura was small and fine-boned, but Dr Murdoch had a stronger frame around which her clothes hung in a confused drapery of colour.

But despite her appalling dress-sense — my God! training shoes! — she still had that lobster-red mouth and eyes as green as crab-meat.

Several weeks later those eyes fixed on him closely when she returned to him his first essay. They were in her study, a cupboard of a room with one high window and too much paper. Volumes of books he had never read stood in piles on the floor and spilled under the chairs.

In the confined space of the study her perfume was strong and sweet. Suddenly he felt just the same as when he had walked over the hill to find the earth peeled back and he was visited by the same overwhelming determination to participate in an uncovering.

She turned to him, put down her pen, and smiled.

He recalled with pleasure the clink of the trowel the first time he'd encountered the buried rim of a samian pot, but he was a careful uncoverer and they did not become lovers until the following summer.

By then he had waited longer than he would have liked but it had been a slow process, peeling away the mantle of her knowledge until he came to the final internal shell. Which turned out to be so soft he should have been warned.

Arthropods periodically shed their carapace and grow one anew.

Should you catch a soft-shelled crab you must throw it back until it is older because most of its energy is going into building another shell and the meat will be thin and tasteless. In Ruth's case, Simon had been gone less than two years at that time and her new shell was still in progress.

So even after Alex had taken off her clothes and entered her delicate body he found this was not the end. With the intuition of a practised uncoverer he realised that there were other things to be known here, and that even though she had given herself to him on a hot summer's afternoon while her daughter slept in the next room, she was not yet in love with him.

So he took up his special knives.

He sent her flowers he could ill-afford. Wrote poetry and copied it onto hand-made scented paper. Woke her at six in the morning with urgent phone-calls.

She began to weaken, but still he cut deeper.

He talked of leaving his wife. That seemed like the next thing to offer her, the next layer to be removed in the archaeology of an affair. It is usually said at some point. It is simply part of the process.

So he was shocked when, at this promise, his knife slid in deep and fast and stuck like Excalibur.

Suddenly she held him away no longer. In offering her everything — his marriage, his devotion, his future — he had finally convinced her.

She threw herself on the point of his blade, and was lost.

Exultantly, he cleaned his special knives and put them away. The job was done. He had found the kernel, the dead man's fingers, the fleshy seeds hidden in the bitter yellow of the pomegranate.

And she began to ask when? when will you leave her?

As the weeks passed he kept his knives hidden though she cried to have them back, to feel their sharpness again. But he knew that there would no longer be anything left for him to discover.

He made a few half-hearted attempts to sew up the wounds he had caused, then finally gave his excuses. After leaving her house for the last time he called in at the market and bought himself a fine live lobster to cook for the family supper.

Mullet provided a very unusual source of entertainment in Ancient Rome. The live fish were brought to the dinner table in containers, then the water emptied out and the evening's spectacle began.

In its death agony the mullet changes colours — a phenomenon in fact quite common amongst fish but one which is perhaps particularly visual in the case of mullet which changes from red to ochre to green before turning the pale and uninteresting beige tone which signifies death.

Once the corpses became dull and colourless the Romans declared the exhibition to be at an end, and the fish were taken back to the kitchen and cooked for general consumption.

Alex had been a painful and humiliating episode in Ruth's past history, but she prided herself on the belief that he was long-forgotten, and indeed it was only when Julie seemed to be drifting away from her that Ruth felt herself gasping once more at the ghostly cut of loneliness.

Back to Northumberland. When they drove away from the hotel the following day Ruth decided against mentioning her disappointment of the previous evening, mainly because she could not identify any particular subject for discussion. As far as she could tell, their relationship had simply undergone a subtle sea-change and she would have to wait to discover more.

Julie, of course, knew why things were different, and she was unusually quiet in the front passenger seat as she re-memoried the boy with the tattoo on his arm.

They would not be coming back to that town. She had thought of suggesting they spend one more night there, but then she decided against it. Who was he anyway? Just someone who had helped her to slip into womanhood. A solitary and anonymous ship passing in the night.

She gave little thought to her mother, except to observe that this was one momentous event they would not be sharing. On the night of the incident in the country lay-by she had begun a separate life and although sometimes she yearned to have a giggle with Ruth about her exploits she knew there was no way that her mother would laugh at such shared confidences.

Ruth negotiated a roundabout and looked for road signs, unaware that Julie was watching her not in the way that a child regards her Mum, but as one woman studies another. The daughter could find no trace of sensuality in the tiny lines around Ruth's pursed lips. Instead she saw an ageing celibate being, completely asexual, a woman whose body had been rejected by her husband and was no longer required by anyone else. The hands on the wheel were blotched and wrinkled, the nails uneven and dirty.

First she felt pity for her mother, then anger at her father for leaving them both alone quickly followed by sudden terror that some man might do the same to her one day. There and then she determined that she would defend herself whatever the cost, and never lose control. She vowed never to give herself, but only to receive. Ruth had been weak — here the pity turned to disdain — she'd wanted too much and given too much, but Julie would do neither.

It would be lonely, this separate life, but there was nothing for it. She would have to be careful about what she said from now on. In fact, probably for ever. But she was more used to keeping inconsequential secrets about broken crockery or bad school marks, and to feeling inevitably relieved when the truth finally came out. As it always did.

This was the first big secret, the first adult secret, she'd ever had, and the necessity of it was hard to come to terms with.

And so they arrived at Seahouses, with Julie thinking about the adulthood ahead of her and Ruth feeling the loss of motherhood behind her. It was fortunate that the boats were running that morning and they would be able to shake off their mood with an exhilarating sea-trip.

But this was also to be the day when Ruth found Ruari and decided to keep him forever.

Meeting the wrong man is like stepping into the waves of an ebb tide — you feel the pull of the water beneath your feet and you're drawn to follow it. You know, of course, that when the tide turns you'll glance around to find yourself way out of your depth.

So even as you look at him you can feel the sharp shingle dragging between your toes and it's time to head for the shore above the tide-line.

Sometimes you leave it too late.

Ruth had been pulled out to sea so many times that she was wary of everyone. She'd known men who were too young, too old, too selfish, too kind. Too painful, like Alex. No-one ever seemed right.

But when she saw Ruari it didn't take long to realise that here was just what she needed. It would be painless for both of them. He would never know what she'd taken.

Seahouses is a small seaside town clinging to the edge of the northern fishing grounds. The chip shops and the amusement arcades make their money from Newcastle excursionists, but the real attractions of this remote resort are the boat-trips — north to Holy Island or eastward to the Farnes, where Grace Darling once ventured across the raging ocean and became a hero just by being a woman.

Like thousands of tourists before her, Ruth yearned to taste the salt-spray on her lips, so they bought their tickets and waited on the harbour wall to board the boat.

They sat at the bows and bounced along the waves until the mainland became a thin dark line and the Farnes loomed up in front. Once anchorites had scourged themselves on these flat and barren rocks — now a reclusive bird-watcher was the sole inhabitant. They saw his single house resting in its eyrie on the cliffs, then passed on between the islands to watch a colony of Atlantic seals.

The boatman cut the engine and took up his microphone to tell them about the indigenous wildlife, his soft tones crackling through the speaker. Ruth watched him as he stood behind the damp glass of his cabin and his features seeped into her heart.

She was shocked at the way she found his face so thoroughly hypnotic. Tearing her gaze away to watch the seals diving and dipping in the water, she wondered if they had crept ashore and cast off their skins to become human for a night, and whether he was the issue of their pleasure.

Or maybe it was mermaids who had given birth to this sea-washed creature of the deeps.

He had the rosy skin of a red-haired man, scrubbed pink with salt, his cheeks closely-shaven and dimpled-soft. Above his wide nose and broad cheekbones lay a pair of deep-set hazel eyes, and as he spoke she noticed his mouth was too small, his teeth sharp and widely-spaced. His high forehead led to a mass of hair, not red as expected but damp blonde, and although his features were coarse they were softened by the pebble-smooth dimpled pinkness of his skin.

But she had no desire at all to attract his attention. She just wanted to drink him in and save him up for later.

Suddenly a voice addressed him over the ship-to-shore radio. The boatman, it seemed, was called Ruari. She liked the name immediately.

After a short exchange on the radio, he re-started the engine and they set off for the Longstone Rock. Grace Darling's home.

He landed the craft and invited the trippers to visit the lighthouse, remembering to smile as he stood on the tiny quay to help them out of the rocking boat. Ruth took his hand, and although it was the only time she ever touched him, her skin imprinted him on its memory and over the years it would pass the knowledge on to new cells as they grew, until her whole body knew him by name. A deeply-padded hand, warm and firm.

She was the last to leave the boat, and he grinned at her politely before turning away to open a bubbling can of Coke. She hurried to catch up with the others.

The Longstone has always resisted civilisation and Grace's family never succeeded in planting a garden there. They grew their vegetables and kept their livestock on Brownsman Island, one of the Outer Farnes. Brownsman is desolate and bleak, but at least it's capable of sustaining some vegetation whereas Longstone is almost completely covered at high tide and nothing grows there but seaweed.

Grace Darling and her family, lighthouse keepers, were transferred from Brownsman to the newly-built light on Longstone in 1826. Every day they rowed their coble through the perilous channels between the islands to tend the gardens and the flocks left marooned on the Outer Farnes.

On Longstone a narrow path leads the way through shallow pools towards the red-striped tower, where one of the keepers waited to show the trippers around.

Ruth tagged on to the end as they passed through the engine room and began to climb the coiled stairs. There was no sign of Julie. Probably she had pushed her way to the front of the group.

The steps were steep and Ruth was distracted by an image of the boatman's seascaped features which persisted in floating ahead of her until they came to the final part of the climb — a short vertical staircase. Then he disappeared for a moment, only to rematerialise in the two enormous light bulbs powering the lamp.

They gathered in a circle around the mechanism while the

keeper described its workings and as he talked Ruth suddenly realised that Julie was absent from the little group. She was instantly filled with fear — perhaps the child had got into difficulties somewhere around the wave-washed rock.

From her vantage point at the top of the tower she looked around but could see no Julie — only a fisherman recasting his line. The mainland was just visible beyond the dark choppy sea, whilst in the other direction she could see distant tankers gliding along the horizon. Directly below, glossy waves caressed the rocks and engulfed them before sliding back to the deeps. But no sign of Julie.

'Excuse me!' She pushed past the keeper and lowered herself backwards down the steep steps to the engine-room and hurried outside.

'Julie?'

Only the sea-birds.

'Julie! Where are you?'

Her voice tightened as she fell into panic. Despite her romantic passion for the ocean, it also terrified her. Drowning is so easy. So quick. One step too far, one slip from a rock...

On the 7th of September 1838 the steamship Forfarshire struck Big Harcar on the Farnes, and almost immediately broke in two. It had foundered less than four hundred yards from the Longstone Light, from which Grace Darling and her father put to sea in a rescue attempt which would make Grace famous throughout the British Isles.

She was twenty-two years old at the time. Her brothers were sleeping ashore that night, leaving Grace and her elderly parents alone on Longstone. Nothing unusual in that. But during the hours of darkness a tremendous storm arose and drove the passing steamship onto the rocks. The family first saw the wreck a little before 5am, but nothing could be done until daylight two hours later and even then, despite the fact that the ship was so close, an approach through the gale-swept sea looked to be impossible.

They decided to row their twenty-foot coble round through the southern passage, double the distance but protected at least from the full fury of the open sea. Mrs Darling helped to push the boat into the water, and Grace and her father set off through the roaring surf in the hope that there would be enough survivors to help them row back against the tide.

The Forfarshire had carried sixty-three people. While the Darling family waited helplessly for daylight, nearly all had drowned, and when the rescuers finally reached the reef they found only nine still alive, including a woman holding in her arms the bodies of her two children. It took two trips to carry everyone to the safety of the lighthouse.

Two hours later the survivors were joined on the Longstone by the crew of the North Sunderland lifeboat, too late for the rescue and now marooned by the gale.

Another nine survivors were later found adrift and picked up by a sloop bound for Tynemouth.

And Grace became a superstar.

Despite the fact that every day all around the country men risked their lives on the sea, Grace was lifted up as a national heroine because women were not expected to do this sort of thing.

The Times of 1838 enthused *Is there in the whole field of history, or of fiction even, one instance of female heroism to compare for one moment with this?*

The poet Wordsworth dubbed her *A guardian spirit, sent from pitying heaven.*

Grace was invited to appear at the Adelphi Theatre in "WRECK AT SEA", and Batty's Equestrian Circus in Edinburgh tried to persuade her to make a public appearance.

She declined both.

Plagued by tourists, requests for locks of her hair, portrait painters and poets, she must have been at a loss to know what all the fuss was about. She had grown up on those barren rocks and travelled regularly between the islands in fair weather and foul. Her hands were calloused from the oars and her complexion weathered with salt. She knew that to the bourgeoisie of the south she would have appeared a roughened, inarticulate peasant, no stranger to the elements.

And, of course, she had seen drownings all her life.

'Hi!'

'Julie! I was really worried. I thought you'd...'

'What? Fallen off this pathetic lump of rock?' Julie wrenched a pebble from the sea-weed and hurled it disrespectfully into the snarling waves. 'For God's sake! Can't I go anywhere without you?

I was just having a look round.'

'Don't you want to go up the light-house?'

'No. It's boring. I was hunting for shells, actually. Look at these...'

'Yes.' replied Ruth, hardly glancing at the handful. Now that her panic had subsided she was angry with herself and with Julie. 'Very nice. Just don't wander off again will you? We could have gone without you.'

'Bloody hell Mum! I'm not a kid.' The St Christopher medal lay warm against her throat. 'Just leave me alone.'

'And where are you going now?'

'Back to the boat. Where do you think?'

As Julie stumped off, her mother sank to the safety of the nearest rock. There seemed to be no way to communicate any more. They had evolved into a pair of islands separated by dangerous waters, and even their shouts were drowned by the wind-blown waves.

She gazed into the deep pool beside her. Longstone seemed to be more liquid than solid and in the clear water she could see dozens of baby jelly-fish floating like upturned puddings, knocking into each other then drifting apart again. There was no sign of a parent jelly-fish.

Eventually everyone returned to the boat, and Ruari manoeuvred them backwards until they were facing the open sea again. Then he revved the engine and they began to fly out between the deadly rocks towards the island bar.

As they passed over the bar the swell of the open sea caught the vessel and threw it into the air, sending a wave slashing back over the bows and into the faces of the passengers. They squealed with delight, but two people promptly threw up over the side.

Ruth and Julie, wet through to the skin, forgot their quarrel and beamed at each other. Ruth put an arm around her daughter's shoulders and held her firmly so that, for once, the girl could forget her fear of the sea.

They clung together, screaming with wild joy, as the boat rocked and thumped across the deep water. This was better than any fairground wild-water ride. Their cheeks glowed, warmed and flushed with excitement, quickly drying the spray into faint maps of salt, and they clasped so close that each could smell the seaweed odour of the other's skin.

Behind them Ruari sat impassively at the wheel as the spray flew against the glass of the cabin.

When they reached the harbour Julie jumped off first and put out her hand to help her mother out of the boat.

Forgiven.

'Come on. Let's get something to eat. I'm starving.'

And walking along the pier arm-in-arm with her daughter, Ruth forgot to look back at the boatman for a last time. But it didn't matter, because she had already sealed him like a ship in a bottle and, like Captain Cat stirring in his bunk, he would nuzzle up to her in dreams and remind her of a time when her skin was salt-toasted brown, her hair sticky with brine, and her feet smoothed by the pull of shingle on cold beaches.

And although she had wanted every other man in her life to be a harbour, this one would never come in to land, but would rest becalmed on the ocean for a long, long time.

They found a small cafe and sat down at a table near the window. Tired and hungry, Julie threw her wet coat under the table and grabbed the menu.

'God! I'm famished! I'll have haddock and chips and some bread and butter.'

Ruth tried, but could not disguise her distaste.

'Must you eat fish?'

'What do you mean?' retorted Julie. 'You eat it.'

Her mother looked around the cafe at the decorative nets and lobster pots. Decorative but deadly.

'I'm giving it up. I was thinking, out there on the boat, that fishing is so savage.'

'Oh well, that's life. God, I'm hungry.'

'No, listen. I've just realised how easy it is to kill them. I mean, it doesn't take much of a man to do it, does it? They don't fight back. They don't scream. They're completely helpless.'

'Yeah, but they don't feel anything, do they? I mean, they don't feel pain.'

'How do you know? Come on, tell me how you know that?'

'Well... oh for God's sake, they're just not like us.'

'I see. So just because something's not like you it's okay to kill it, is it? It makes me so... just think of those men who spend their Sundays sitting on a river-bank in the hope of capturing some living being only to rip the hook out of its mouth and throw it back again... it makes me sick.'

29

'The fact is,' replied Julie nastily, 'they're probably just trying to get away from their nagging wives. In fact, I seem to remember that Dad used to go fishing now and again...'

'And what's that supposed to mean?'

'Nothing. I'm sorry. Forget it.'

'Yes. Why don't we? You don't know anything about your father, so don't try to pretend you do. Right? Let that be an end to it.' Ruth straightened her shoulders and consulted the menu. 'I'll just have a plain salad and a baked potato.'

She felt weary and irritable. The adrenalin of the boat-ride had deserted her and now she was ready for a good lunch and a long nap. She'd enjoyed the return trip and had hoped to maintain the friendly atmosphere, but it seemed impossible to talk to Julie about anything these days.

She made one more effort towards peace.

She asked 'Did you enjoy the ride?'

'It was great!' Julie smiled pax, remorseful after her unpleasant jibes. 'Really exciting, flying over the waves. I wasn't even scared, either.' She paused. 'Shame about the boat-man though.'

Ruth raised her head. 'Why?'

'I thought we'd get a really handsome one. You know. With tattoos and all that. Been around the world and a girl in every port.'

I touched a tattoo last night, she thought to herself.

The memory made her fingers ache.

But she looked up to see that Ruth had a rather strange smile on her face — one Julie had not seen before. A very private smile.

'He wasn't so bad!' she was saying.

'Mum! He was nearly half your age!'

Ruth rescued herself quickly. 'Oh — I didn't mean in that way. Good Lord, I'm past looking at men. I've had my share of falling in love.'

Julie regarded her closely. 'Who else have you been in love with then, apart from Dad?'

'Well,' Ruth smiled. 'The first time, I was younger than you are now.'

'Never!'

'Yes, really. I was fourteen.'

A tall girl with eyes painted city black brought them their meal and they fell quiet for a moment as they ate. Julie dissected her fish and began a tidy row of bones and skin on the edge of her plate, while Ruth tried not to think about the haddock dozing on the sea-bed.

'Is any kind subject to rape like fish?'

John Donne

In February the North Sea is noisy with the sound of haddock love-calls.

They live close to the bottom, a thousand feet down, feeding on crustaceans, shellfish, and sea urchins.

When the females begin to sense the end of winter they get ready to spawn and the males prepare to fight.

Approaching his rival the male haddock produces a series of faster and faster double-syllable knocks which rise to the hum of an angry bee as he chases his opponent and tries to ram him into defeat. When he has had enough and wants to make his escape his tone changes to a pulsing grunt of submission and the fight is over.

The field left clear for him, the victor approaches the female who is wandering unconcerned over the sea-bed. She makes no reply as he swims around her in ever-tightening circles, his knocks almost following the electro-cardiogram of a regular human heartbeat. The knocks get faster and faster until he is revving like an engine, and his skin begins to blush darkly until she finally, voicelessly, begins to spawn.

Now he falls silent as he curls onto her back in close embrace and they swim upwards together, shedding behind them a smoky trail of eggs and milt.

For fifteen days the eggs keep company with the plankton floating near the surface of the sea. Once hatched, the tiny haddock fry take cover for several months amongst the trailing tentacles of jelly fish until they are large enough to make the journey to the ocean floor.

Of course, there are dangers. Inshore currents drive the fry into estuaries and leave them stranded. Many of them become food for other fish. But even once they have grown sufficiently to rejoin a shoal on the sea-bed they are still not safe.

Gill nets are made of fine monofilaments which hang down from the surface to the sea-bottom. Thin and grey, they are invisible to fish, who swim into them and become trapped by their gills. They hang there, the net biting into their flesh, until the boat returns to pull them upwards a thousand feet into the

31

drowning air.

Wrenched free from the sharp netting they lie in wide-eyed surprise amongst hundreds of other gill-trapped creatures and torn-limbed crustaceans while the reapers of the sea select the best of the squirming, gasping, bloody heap then throw back the bulk of the catch. Most of the jettisoned haul will be already dead anyway.

Seine netters kill differently. Gill nets are slow grotesque curtains of death, but seine nets trawl an instant bagful of everything then dump it on the deck leaving the glassy bodies to twist in the agonies of the bends, their internal cavities pumped up like balloons by the rapid decompression.

It is not known what sound the haddock makes at these times. To human ears the death of a fish is a silent art, as graceful as a lazy yawn.

Julie took a bite of her bread and returned to the subject of romance. There were things she needed to know.

'Mum — how did you know you were in love?'

Ruth chewed on her lettuce and hoped it couldn't feel anything. She grinned.

'I thought you knew.'

'Not really.'

'Don't worry,' replied her mother. 'You'll get a boyfriend soon.' She surveyed her daughter's smooth cheeks. 'You're very pretty, you know. Much prettier than I was at your age.'

'So — did you kiss him and everything? What was his name?'

'Of course I kissed him! That's what you do with boyfriends isn't it?'

'Did you go out with him for long?'

'Well we went around together for about six months... but I thought it was for ever. Do you know —' she stole a triangle of bread and butter from Julie's plate and smiled at the memory. '— at one point I was even worried that I'd have to marry him!'

'Why?' asked Julie in a shocked voice 'Were you pregnant?'

'Oh no!'

Deep water coming up.

'What I mean is, I had this idea that since we were in love, we'd have to get married eventually. I mean, I thought that was what people did.'

'But you slept with him though?'

'Julie, I was only fourteen. Of course I didn't.'

(But she did.)

'So you were a virgin when you married Dad?'

'Julie! This is your mother you're talking to.'

'Come on Mum. Were you or not?'

What are you supposed to say when your fifteen year old daughter asks you these things? Ruth did what many of us do, despite our good intentions. She made subtle alterations to the fabric of history in the hope that her good example might influence her daughter's moral code. She said

'I didn't sleep with anyone before I met your father. Do you want a pudding?'

Julie ignored the question. Instead, she concentrated on re-arranging fish-bones with the point of her knife.

'Dawn's done it.'

'Done what?'

'Had it off with someone.'

'Don't say 'had it off' Julie, it sounds so coarse.'

'Had sexual intercourse', then. With a boy.'

Ruth put down her knife and fork firmly.

'Well, she's evidently not the right friend for you then, is she? I think you'd better find yourself another crowd to go around with if that's the case.'

'They're all like that, Mum.'

'Don't raise your voice. And don't be ridiculous. They can't all be "like that" '.

'It's true,' answered Julie desperately. Why couldn't she be more understanding? 'Things have changed since your day.'

'I hope you haven't...?'

Julie met her mother's eyes. 'No. No, I haven't. Honestly.'

'Well — your friends. Don't they worry about AIDS? I mean, when I was a girl you just had to think about getting pregnant, but now it's not just that is it? I mean, you could *die* Julie.'

My God. She was right. Julie hadn't thought about that at all. She remembered the graveyard eyes in those TV adverts. Had he looked healthy? He'd been a bit pale, but then it was almost dark... she wiped her mouth and changed the subject.

'Where are we going this afternoon?'

'I don't know yet. Listen Julie,' Ruth picked up the menu and studied the design on the cover. Dolphins. Embossed in gold. 'If you find a boyfriend and you start thinking about — making love

33

— you will talk to me first won't you? There are a lot of things to be taken into consideration these days...'

'Yes Mum.'

'It's just that it's an important step to take. You need to think about it, to decide if he's the right person. There's more to love than just sex you know.'

'I don't know why you're giving me all this when I haven't even got a boyfriend.'

'I know, darling. But these things have to be talked about. And I know you won't do anything silly. End of conversation, OK?'

'I need to go to the toilet.'

The lavatory was tiny and smelled of pine woods and urine. Julie locked herself in, banged down the toilet-seat, and sat down.

Why hadn't Ruth noticed anything? She'd been given every chance to push Julie into an admission of last night. She was burning to talk about it, to tell what she'd done, tell about the boy with a St. Christopher around his neck,

— and how much she'd longed to get rid of the stupid virginity which set her aside from Dawn and the other girls

— and how she'd wanted a holiday romance but all she'd got was a one-night stand under the bushes of an anonymous inland town

— and he hadn't used a condom as far as she knew and she wasn't sure if she could tell anyway if he had or not

— and never mind how nice he was, when he was on top of her his eyes glazed over like a cat staring at an invisible ghost

— and that even though she'd said yes she felt totally and utterly used

— and she wanted to ask what was the point of it all

— and half of her felt just the same as before while the other half was filled with dread because now there was no looking back

— and when someone she really liked, someone *worthy,* did ask her out he would discover that she wasn't a virgin and then he'd hate her

34

— and how it was all the fault of that boy in the lay-by, well he wasn't a boy he was a man, and she'd been completely stupid to think she was in his league

— because that night she'd decided she'd better learn quick or she'd look an idiot

— and she'd pretended to be someone she wasn't because somehow she'd got caught in this trap where your body needed to qualify and pass exams too and so she'd rushed to get it over with and now all she felt was empty and cheap and not sophisticated at all

— and that Dawn probably wouldn't even believe her when she told her about the tattooed boy but she couldn't tell Ruth because Ruth would never understand

— and how Julie was weighed down by the fullness of private experience which she could never properly convey to anyone so she supposed that counted as adulthood

— and that if Dad had been around she would have got used to boys by now, and the way they're so different

— and she just wished she'd never done it, and that Ruth could make it OK again, but that was impossible.

When she went back to the table her mother had ordered chocolate gateau as a special treat but Julie was overtaken by mysterious tears and could not eat it.

Alex again

Alex had made the last of his excuses just before the start of the new Autumn Term. His orderly mind would not allow one excavation to run over into the next, and he knew that the second year of his degree would take up all of his time.

So he tidied up as best he could.

He booked a baby-sitter for the twins and drove Laura to a riverside pub. There, sitting in the last of the September sun, he disclosed to her that his first year's study had encompassed more than reading books and writing essays. Of course, she had long suspected this to be the case but she was relieved to hear his confession at last. She, too, was of a pragmatic turn of mind and she had already planned a secret timetable which carried open options on his potential for redemption.

Laura was an old-fashioned woman. She valued her marriage above most other things and she was prepared to work hard to keep it. Alex's mother had told her long ago that stoicism and forward planning would be required if the relationship was to work on Laura's terms, and she had taken the advice much to heart.

Over the years they had been together — nearly ten, counting from the day they met — she had grown used to her husband's succeeding obsessions. First it had been car-mechanics, then it was cooking. And now, since that fateful camping trip, history.

As far as the anatomy of Alex's fixations went, Ruth had only played a very small part. As Laura had known she would. It was comparable to his flirtation with health foods four years earlier, when he'd spent a year cooking in a macrobiotic restaurant and had insisted that at home too the family should adapt to hiziki and brown rice.

Now history had taken his fancy, and Ruth was just another subject for short-term investigation. But Laura felt somehow certain that having tried his hand once at sexual conquest, he was unlikely to return to it. However, as a careful planner she had always kept in mind that this woman might just possibly have turned out to be a full-blown obsession. So her plan allowed for that too.

Had the affair carried on into the coming term, Laura planned to leave Alex just before the seasonal festivities. Christmas Eve would probably have been the most effective date, with New Year's Day marked down for the reconciliation. Christmas Week on his own would probably be sufficient punishment for his continued infidelity, and anyway the twins would enjoy spending the holiday with their cousins in Kent.

Still, now that the storm had blown over there was no reason why they should not still go away for Christmas in the guise of a complete and happy family. Unbeknown to him, his confession had awarded Alex a secret reprieve. But Laura, of course, would never allow him to find that out.

He took her hand in his across the beer-stained table and

repeated for the sixth time that he was sorry. He was inwardly
relieved she was taking things so calmly, but then he had never
understood women. His mother had made sure of that.

'You know I've always loved you.' he begged. 'And the twins...
you won't leave me will you Laur?'

'Perhaps we should sleep separately for a while,' she replied
stonily. 'I'm not sure I want to... you know... when you've just...'

'I know. I know. I'm sorry. Anything you say.'

Laura evaded his penitent eyes and sipped her sparkling wine.
It fizzed on her tongue.

'Which one is she anyway?' She laughed lightly. 'My rival. What
does she look like?'

Alex was unsure whether to respond to this dangerous line of
questioning, but if Laura was to be placated he had little choice.

'Long dark hair. Quite plump. Not as well-dressed as you...' He
ran his fingers along her cheek seductively, but she drew back
coldly.

'Oh — I think I've seen her — surely you don't mean the tall
woman, Alex — not the scruffy one with the terrible clothes —
hair all over the place — ?'

Sorry Ruth, but he was in no position to defend you. And in
fact he felt rather humiliated because it was true that next to
Laura's polished appearance you were something of an
embarrassment.

'Could be...' he muttered into his beer.

'Hmm...' She withdrew her hand from his.

A silence fell between them. Inside the pub, a fruit machine
rattled out the jack-pot.

Alex felt oppressed, as if a ten ton weight was hovering above
his head. He prepared to dodge the blow...

'Do you want another drink? Or shall we go somewhere else?'
He reached for her empty glass.

Laura wrapped her fingers round it and pulled it towards her.
She caught his eye and held it coldly.

'So. What did you see in her, Alex?'

She was enjoying this opportunity of making him squirm. The
chance seldom arose when she could watch him twist on the end
of a sharp hook, and it would be informative to see his reactions.

'God knows. Honestly. I swear, I've no idea.'

'Oh come on! There must have been something for Christ's
sake! You don't just go out and screw someone else for no reason.'

'Oh, she was just... interesting. She knows things... Oh, I don't

37

know.'

Well I do, thought Laura. I know you better than you do yourself. You were trying to steal from her. You're jealous of her education, of her position. She's got something you haven't.

I know you, she thought.

'Look,' said Alex meekly, disconcerted by her hard gaze. 'Shall we go and sit inside? It's getting chilly out here.'

'OK.'

She'd let him swim free for a little while now.

They found a table near the log fire and Alex bought more drinks.

When they had settled again, Laura smiled.

'Oh, I meant to tell you. Someone came into the shop with a card to put in the window. He wants to sell his word-processor.'

'Oh?'

'I thought it might come in handy for you. It's quite cheap too. But of course, that was before all this happened...'

Alex jumped straight off the hook and into the keep net. His eyes lit up.

'I must admit I'd been thinking about one...'

'Mind you, they take a long time to learn.' Her sharp regular teeth bit into a packet of dry roasted peanuts, releasing a noxious odour into the air between them. 'He said he ended up staying in all last winter until he got the hang of it.'

'So why is he selling it then?'

'Wants a better one, he said.'

'Well,' mused Alex, feeling the walls of the net tighten around him and rather appreciating their security. 'I don't mind staying in. I could learn to use it and study at the same time. Type up my notes, essays, that sort of thing...'

'And you could teach the kids too!'

An added small penance. Fair enough. He would accept it.

'Why not?' Suddenly he felt the weight swing away from his skull. 'I'll go and see it tomorrow shall I?'

Laura nodded her assent as she rolled a peanut around inside her petite mouth and savoured the salt. She was glad everything was settled.

Long ago in the North there lived two sisters. The elder loved the shore, and would walk along the beach in foul weather and fair.

In the winter she planted her feet firmly on the shingle to confront the waves head on, and her power was such that they never splashed her but always stopped short of her toes. In the summer she took off her robe and swam naked above the shell-covered sea-bed as the northern sun tanned her bare shoulders to a tawny sheen.

The younger sister, on the other hand, was a child of the fields and hills. Her favourite season was autumn, when leaves covered the floors of the forests and the corn stood tall and ripe in the furrow. She loved the fine golden dust of the threshing-room, and the bright colours of the berried hedgerows.

They grew up together happily, each with her own domain in the natural world — one sister with her feet firmly on land, the other ever dreaming of ships.

Then one day a beautiful knight came to the cliff-top castle where they lived and although both immediately fell in love with him he courted only the elder sister for she was the family heir. But despite his protestations it was clear to everyone that truly he preferred the younger.

> *He courted one with gloves and rings*
> *but he loved the other above all things*

One day the two sisters were standing on the cliffs watching the distant ships far out at sea, when the weather suddenly turned around and a furious gale blew up from the water. The elder, seeing her opportunity and feeling this must be a gift from her beloved sea, was stricken by a quickening desire to act and before she could stop herself she had grabbed the other by the waist and thrown her over the rocks and into the roaring waves below.

> *sometimes she sank, sometimes she swam,*
> *crying "sister! reach to me your hand!"*

But the sea bore her on, still crying out, and the elder sister hardened her heart and turned away.

After the usual period of mourning the wedding plans were made. The bereaved knight concealed his sorrow, weeping only when at private prayer, but the elder sister was so solicitous of his secret grief that he came to admire her and soon the memory of his lover began to dim. The elder sister wept too, but she was so numbed with guilt that her heart had turned to ice and even the desperate passion she had felt for the knight when her rival was alive had diminished to no more than a faint cold pulse.

A few days before the wedding two minstrels were walking along the shore when they saw a skeleton wash up in the waves. The fishes of the deep had cleaned the bones of flesh but the scalp still clung to the skull, and long strands of yellow hair tangled with ribbons of dark-green weed. To their surprise they were not afraid of the corpse, but were instead strangely drawn to it. Even as they watched, the sections of the skeleton fell away from each other until only the breastbone remained, glowing with traces of marine phosphor. They felt somehow bidden to collect it up, and from the sternum and some strands of hair they built the most serene and melodious harp.

> *they made a harp of her breastbone*
> *whose sound would melt a heart of stone*

On the morning of the ceremony the minstrels entered the Great Hall to greet their friends. But as they proudly set down their new instrument it suddenly began to play of its own accord. The collected company gathered round to hear its eerie tones, but when the bride and groom arrived the sound was mysteriously transposed into a mellifluous human voice which both immediately recognized as that of the dead younger sister. As the harp began to tell its story of treacherous violence and deceit, the older sister ran loudly weeping down to the shore where she fell into the arms of a single tall wave which collected her up and carried her away to the kingdoms of Neptune below.

And even as the murderer sank to her watery grave the harp glowed once more with phosphorous and the younger sister stood smiling before the weeping company.

But even though she was returned to life again, she would never forget the year she had spent beneath the waves. The skin of her back was found to be finely-patterned with rainbow fish-scales and although she married the knight and had many children, to her dying day she swam every evening in the sea.

Some say she met her sister in the deeps and there they became young and innocent again, as if their lives had not yet been tainted by the passion and sorrow of men.

Ruth withdrew to tend her wounds.

As Autumn gave way to a mild winter she started to clear her garden of dead annuals, putting the longer-living plants to rest beneath piles of leafy mulch. She cut cornus stems to ground level in the hope that their new bright red branches would cheer her up through the coming snows and then, along with the dahlias and chrysanthemums, she too died down for the season.

Julie was six years old. School had become a familiar routine, and she plodded through the gates each weekday morning carrying a garish pink plastic satchel which was the envy of the other girls. It was one of many presents recently bestowed on her by her mother.

Ruth had surfaced from the bloodwash of Alex's knives to a realisation that she had given Julie precious little attention over the past year. The raw torments of her affair had twisted her from joy to depression to irritability, forcing Julie to learn the self-protection of lying low. Ruth was shocked when she finally noticed that all of the brightness had been knocked out of the child. Julie had become sombre and withdrawn, and Ruth's moodiness and detachment were the only things to blame.

But first came October, when she reached the very bottom of her despair.

Term began, and she saw Alex several times, but he kept his distance and did not stop to speak. His cool smile and absent eyes were humiliatingly painful.

Through a mechanistic force of will she survived each day long enough to collect Julie from the child-minder, but once she reached the safety of home the tension was released and she dumped the child in front of the TV, a tray of dinner on her lap, before slumping into a testy silence.

Each night Julie was fed and watered, after which Ruth gritted her teeth to listen dutifully to her daughter's reading practise.

'Rog..er....Red...Hat.... what's that word, Mummy?'

'Went. Roger Red Hat went.'

'Roger...Red...Hat.........went....to.....see....his...'

'Friend. Roger Red Hat went to see his friend. How much more is there?'

'Only two pages.' Julie looked up at Ruth's whitened lips and asked carefully 'Do you want me to stop now?'

'No. No. Let's just get on. Roger Red Hat went to see his friend....'

'Bil...Bil....Billy.....Black Hat....'

41

'Blue, Julie. It's Billy Blue Hat. Roger Red Hat went to see his friend Billy Blue Hat. Look, I think we've done enough for tonight now, don't you? I've got a bit of a headache actually. You'd better get ready for bed.'

'But you said I could have a bubble bath tonight.'

'Did I? When?'

'In the car. You said you'd run me a nice deep bubble bath and you'd sit on the edge and talk to me. You did, Mum.'

'Oh. Well, I'm not sure I've got the time now. Tell you what, you have a bath while I wash up the dinner things.'

'Oh Mum!' whined the child, 'I don't want to do it on my own!'

'Julie...' An ominous warning sounded in Ruth's voice.

Sometimes Julie forgot that it was not a good idea to make demands on her mother, especially when she 'had a headache'.

'It's not fair!' she shrilled.

'Right! That's it! No bath and straight to bed!'

Ruth clattered back her chair and rose to her feet until she towered over her daughter. Her eyes had turned into black points of rage and her hands shook as her brain fizzed with sudden irrational fury.

Julie stared at her in dread. This was by no means the first occasion when she had seen her mother so crazed with anger, but every time it was equally terrifying.

'I've had enough!' Ruth spluttered. Drops of spittle formed at the corners of her mouth.

'I work all day to get money to buy you all this stupid crap,' she grabbed the pink satchel and threw it across the floor, 'and when I come home for some peace and quiet all you do is hassle me. Bubble baths! Food! Reading books...'

She sunk back into her chair and held her head in her hands.

'I can't stand it!' she sobbed.

This sentence was the familiar signal for Julie to quietly disappear.

First she moved ghost-like around the room replacing the books and pens scattered from the flying satchel. She put away Roger Red Hat, then crept upstairs and got herself ready for bed in the hope that by the time she had put on her pyjamas Ruth would have calmed down enough to come and tuck her in.

But her skirt was stiffly buttoned and she had to struggle to undo the loops by herself, ripping a delicate nail down the edge in the process. She did not cry out, but sucked her finger in silence until the pain subsided. Eventually after much effort she got the skirt off, then struggled out of her t-shirt, vest and pants. She unlaced her shoes and slipped off her socks, laying them all neatly together on the bed-side chair.

Being careful of her sore finger she dragged open a drawer but could find no clean night-clothes. There were none in the airing cupboard either.

Cold and naked, she stood at the top of the stairs and listened.

Silence.

In desperation she pulled a dirty nightdress from amongst the washing in the linen basket and put it on. It smelled horrible, but there was no other option but to wear it.

She washed and brushed her teeth, listened again for a moment at the top of the stairs, then climbed into bed beside the blue teddy her father had given her for her second birthday. She cuddled it and waited for Ruth to come and kiss her goodnight.

But Ruth could not face the journey up to that solitary little bedroom.

She had remained still, listening to her daughter's progress upstairs as she got herself ready for bed, but although her heart ached with guilt and sorrow she dared not go up. Despite her remorse at her appalling behaviour in front of this defenceless child, she knew that she had not yet regained enough self-control to face the request for a bed-time story. The words would choke in her throat. She had nothing to give, no more patience, no more love to show. They were all locked up in her embattled heart and she could not go upstairs.

She waited for half an hour, by which time she was sure Julie would be fast asleep and no demands would be made. Then she crept up to the room.

The bare window stared cold and black with night.

As she pulled the curtains closed she saw the tidy pile of discarded clothes and the little scuffed red shoes on the top.

Then she sat on the floor beside the bed of the sleeping child and watched Julie's pale face, the blue teddy clutched in one small hand. Ruth felt her heart push up into her throat and tears filled her eyes as she looked at her only child, abandoned and ignored. Ruth's fault. Ruth's guilt.

And this was not the first vigil she had kept here in this room.

How many, many times she had sat beside this small bed with its cartooned quilt and longed to wake Julie up there and then, to wrap her in her arms and promise that she would never, ever, lose her temper again. She wanted forgiveness and forgetting and a new start.

But it is not possible to begin again with children. Words said can never be unsaid. Actions cannot be undone. A child's love for its parent is huge and almost unbreakable.

Almost.

It endures indignities and insults, and although it may bury itself deep it still remains intact, if contorted by experience. It is a dependant's love, a prisoner's love, not freely given but awarded by bio-chemical chance.

And a child's affection cannot easily be diminished, but it can be trained until it turns into a snarling wolf of resentment.

Ruth did not wake Julie up.

What could she have said to change things?

After a time she wiped her eyes and rose to pull the quilt tighter around the sleeping child. But as she leaned across to kiss that small wan forehead the sudden action woke Julie from her dream and her eyes sprang open in terror:

'No Mummy! Don't! I'm sorry!'

Maybe the plea came from inside the dream, and maybe not, but Ruth froze in fear at that blank sleeper's expression. Immediately the child's eyes closed again as she turned muttering into her pillow, and Ruth made her firmest promise yet that she would never hear that cry again.

That night she dreamt she was on trial for custody of her daughter. Teachers, neighbours and friends came to the stand one by one to give evidence against her. Even Simon was there, yet no-one seemed to acknowledge him as an accessory to the crime. She bore the guilt on her own.

Yet, to her shame, all she could do was scream and curse them, furious in the desperate knowledge that she had not matched up to the demands of motherhood.

It's not fair! she yelled.

I'm doing the best I can!

I'm sorry!

I'm sorry!

She felt like a child herself, one who has overstepped the mark and can feel the weight of punishment bearing down upon her, and no escape this time. She pleaded for a second chance, but could offer no proof of her own worth to substantiate it.

And worst of all, there was Julie, condemning in her silence.

Tell them! screamed Ruth.

Tell them I love you really!

44

The child looked at her, but remained dumb. Instead, she hid behind the judge's garments and peered around the court-room.

Then there was a vote.

Ruth left the building even before the count was finished. She knew she was beaten. She waited outside in the street to see her daughter being led away by a wholesome couple, a kind and caring couple, a proper family couple, and Julie did not even look at her as they walked past.

At five a.m. she managed to tear herself out of the nightmare. She lit a cigarette in the darkness to calm her sobs, then climbed out of bed, knelt against the covers, and took a vow of seclusion and devotion to which she was determined to remain true.

From now on, she swore, Julie would be her one priority. No more lovers to disturb the equilibrium, no more overwork to distract Ruth from this cherished childhood which would so soon be over.

In the morning she rose first and ran to hug Julie when she came into the kitchen. The surprised child rested in her mother's arms, yet ready for flight, and smelling of sleep and dirty linen.

After breakfast they drove to a garden centre to spend money, and by the end of the day Ruth had planted a thorny wall of pink roses all around the house and garden.

It would be more than ten years before Julie could cut herself out again.

Some species of African Lungfish can survive even when their pond dries up completely. In poorly oxygenated stagnant water, they switch to breathing air, using their large swim bladder as a lung.

As the water level falls they burrow into the muddy bottom and secrete a cocoon of mucus inside which they remain dormant until the pond refills.

After lunch they left Seahouses and headed for the moors. They needed time away from the pressures of the ocean.

Ruth attributed Julie's tearfulness to her hormones and insisted she curl up under a blanket on the back seat of the car. This done, she was soon asleep and Ruth was left to take stock of the morning on the boat.

Over the years her body had sealed itself against the tide. Slowly, slowly, it had closed its doors against desire.

What else could she have done?

What can you do, when your lover leaves and no-one takes his place? First Simon, then a succession of short affairs, then Alex. After him the days had turned into weeks and months until she suddenly realised that she had been a year alone.

Later, her solitude turned into a hard pain lodged beneath her ribs, and she was forced to slightly adjust her posture to compensate for the change in focus. But since then she had once or twice lowered her defences just enough for someone to deliver a hard blow which left her doubled up in breathless agony once again.

It became obvious to her that something had gone wrong in the chemical world.

In the past there had been some wonderfully enchanted evenings, just like in the song, when she'd met someone and known immediately, even before they'd been introduced, that they would be spending the night together... but then she started to make embarrassing mistakes, and that perplexing chemistry which unites us in love ceased to work.

She began to burst into roaring incandescent flames of desire for men who had no feeling for her. Some chance encounter would spark a series of flickering lights in her mind which then exploded into hysterical passion raging uncontrollably through her thoughts.

For example there was Michael. A single conversation had left Ruth scorched with longing for him. But the more she burned, the more she concealed it. At night she would lie awake making fantasies of how his skin might come alive to her touch, or writing elaborate love letters only to burn them in the hope of casting a spell in the ashes.

But by day, she was radium sealed in a lead-lined flask.

And endless, endless loneliness.

First there was Michael

Michael Sleman had no memory at all of the woman he sat next to at someone's second wedding. The groom was an old friend, and this headlong rush into yet another marriage depressed Michael greatly. For himself, he had adopted a post-marriage policy of sleeping with as many women as possible — just so long as they were under twenty-five with the bodies of children and the minds of acolytes.

Under the influence of too much champagne he gave his views at length to the woman on his right. He did this a) because she was a good listener and b) because he was using what little self-discipline remaining in his drunken state to keep his eyes off his friend's daughter, nearly eighteen and with a tennis-player's waist. The girl had already rebuffed him twice — once when he offered her his arm as they walked into church and again at the bar when she refused to accept a drink from him. The only remaining recourse was to impress her with his erudition by way of a lengthy conversation aimed at the nearest suitable person. So he studiously ignored the small uncaressed breasts beyond the nuptial table-centre and addressed himself to Ruth.

Slugging back yet another glassful he informed her about the position of women in society today — how they could best fulfil themselves and yet still remain true to their essential womanhood (which, as we know, is biologically centred). He fixed his eyes on Ruth's and showed his good manners by remembering to pause every ten minutes or so to allow her to submit a carefully-considered sentence, after which he would smile intelligently, light her cigarette, and continue with his script.

Ruth took note of his prolonged gaze and the brightness of his pupils. She observed that he valued her contribution to the discussion and that he leaned towards her seductively when refilling their glasses.

Her part of the chemistry having been kindled by his intimacy, she waited for the conversation to progress to a less formal level. She asked him questions of a more personal nature, and waited for him to ask her similarly.

Eventually, since he did not ask, she concluded that he was reticent, beaten down by life's hard knocks, and that he needed someone like her to take him out of himself.

She never met him again, but it took several months to dispel his smile, lingering as it did in her mind.

But all he remembered of that day was that his strategy paid off, and within a week the tennis-player returned his service by visiting his bed.

Ruth, of course, had never understood the rules of sport.

...and then there was the handsome lifeguard.

He won't recall it now, but once he helped a woman in a pink bathing suit to find her sunken locker-key.

When he dived beneath the water he noticed that the red varnish on her toenails was badly-chipped and in need of renewal.

Ruth remembered his broad chest and dripping hair, and added his face to her list of possibilities.

Once, years ago, Ruth was leafing through an old natural history book that Simon had left behind, when she came upon some interesting information. It seemed that some fish had a much more interesting sex-life than she'd ever had.

There were, for instance, such things as hermaphrodite fish. You don't need anyone else, because you're both sexes and you can have babies on your own. That sounds pretty good, she thought.

But then again, you might start off as one sex then change to another as you grow up. Don't some humans do that? she mused. Surely there had been something in the Sunday papers about it.

It was interesting that male-turning-into-female only happened in species with no territory to defend. No need to fight, you see. Then there were the female impersonators who avoided potential conflict by pretending to be females and getting to stay in the safety of the nest without doing anything very much to contribute to the fish community.

It occurred to her that such a life would have suited Simon very well, since he was such a natural coward. When their marriage started falling apart he had just run away, straight into someone else's nest, and given up all of his former responsibilities. She'd never been able to decide which was the most humiliating — being deserted by such a man, or the embarrassment of marrying him in the first place. Well, no matter, Julie was certainly better off without her father, though of course she would never believe it.

Ruth had often noticed her secretly observing other Dads when they kicked a football around with their kids. They'd call to her to join in, but she wouldn't. She'd just watch the friendly muddy scrambling and the laughing faces and you could see her adding it all up in her head. Fun. Giggles. Ice-creams. Hugs. If Dad were here he'd be doing that too... but no, he wouldn't actually. Ruth knew that, but how could she tell Julie? Simon had never been the type for rough-and-tumble. He was much more the pipe-behind-the-newspaper sort of father, staid and solid and uncommunicative and bloody boring.

When the baby was born he must have been proud — mustn't he? — but he never changed her nappy or pushed her pram or read her a story. Whatever paternal adoration was going on in his head, he certainly never displayed it. He was a nothing man. Nothingness personified. But Julie had no way of knowing that, and Ruth was not about to tell her. It would seem like betrayal, because in truth she had loved Simon once. It just seemed like an awfully long time ago, that's all.

Upon reaching the moors they discovered that the sea had trailed behind them in the form of clouds and a heavy summer rain began to beat on the roof of the car.

Ruth was disappointed. She had looked forward to pushing a path through the addered bracken but already the landscape was saturated and a walk would be unpleasantly damp.

Julie stirred in the back seat and pulled herself up to look out of the window.

'Oh no! Bloody weather!' she complained. 'What shall we do now?'

'Well,' said Ruth slowly, 'I think the best thing might be to find somewhere to stay for tonight and hope it clears up.'

She felt a sudden sense of adventure.

'We can do what we like!'

'Alright.' Julie couldn't be bothered to argue. 'Whatever you say. I'm going back to sleep.'

They drove on. By now they were travelling without maps.

The road went on and on, with no human habitation in sight.

The road grew steeper, then flattened out. Narrower, then wide enough for two cars.

They passed through broad wet valleys and over high slender mountain roads blue with heather or grey with mist. And still not a single house.

Ruth drew to a halt in a narrow passing-place and searched through her maps, but she could find no trace of the area they were travelling through. She didn't even know whether they were still in England or if they had passed through some invisible boundary and were now on Scottish soil.

She wondered whether to turn back, but there seemed little point. The trip had begun as a leisurely afternoon drive, and she hadn't bothered to look at signposts, so she had no idea where she was anyway.

They were thoroughly lost, and there was nothing to do but keep going forward.

These moors surely can't be so big, thought Ruth, that we won't find anywhere to stay? She tried to reassure herself, but these morose landscapes had always frightened her.

This would never happen on the coast, she grumbled. There at least you can keep the sea in your sights.

As they entered a pass even narrower and darker than the ones before, she began to feel really worried. Perhaps it was time to assess the possibilities of spending the night in the car. At least they had plenty of petrol, but if they broke down out here they would be really in trouble.

Then abruptly she caught sight of a mass of rooftops so unexpected by now that it seemed like a mirage.

Just beyond the pass a large village lay huddled along a narrow river.

There were two public houses and a small hotel called The Mermaid. It was curious to find such a name in a village so far from the ocean.

They were given a warm room, unusually luxurious. It was heavily carpeted in red and had a pair of twin beds with soft herb-scented sheets. Beyond the window there was a small bridge below which a frothy stream carried water down from the moor. Large flat white stones glinted beneath the fast-running current, their paleness heightened by the grey of the sky. Only that morning on the Farnes the salt sun had burned Julie's cheeks, and it was unbelievable that the weather could change so quickly.

Rain still beat against the window and a tall willow tree shimmied in the wind like an enormous green sea-anemone.

It looked as if the downpour would go on all night.

Julie pulled a face.

'Great!' she moaned. 'This place'll a barrel of laughs, I don't think.'

'It's only four o'clock,' said Ruth. 'We can put our feet up before dinner. Then hopefully afterwards it'll be dry enough to walk around the village.'

'But I don't want a rest. I slept in the car.'

'Well, find something to read then.' Ruth took off her jeans and climbed into bed, keeping on her socks for comfort.

'I'm going to have a nap. Will you wake me at six?'

'I suppose so.'

Ruth snuggled under the crisp sheets and, as she always did, hooked her toes over the end of the bed for safety in case she should drift too far in her dreams.

Meanwhile Julie curled up in the one dusty armchair. From where she sat she could see no landscape through the leaded panes of the window, only rain and clouds. The hotel could be floating in the sky and she wouldn't know it. Indeed she wouldn't be surprised if they were suspended in the foggy upper atmosphere. Since last night's love-making beside the lake the ground she stepped on had become less solid, as if she stood on a lavaflow. It seemed to slide along, pulling her with it as they progressed steadily downwards.

'You could die.' Ruth's words.

The graveyard eyes came back to her again. Had he carried death at the end of his penis like a poisoned barb? If so, how long would it be before she found out? She didn't know much about these things.

At school everyone made jokes about condoms, and she had even seen a few blown up like balloons or filled with water and catapulted across the playing-field.

She wondered if her body would waste away; whether she would need a wheelchair; whether she would be shut in an isolation unit where visitors would wear a mask and a gown.

She pictured Ruth standing weeping over her bed-side and felt a nasty thrill of satisfaction. Then another figure floated into view.

It was the ghost of Dad.

Dad with tears on his cheeks like the time before when he had leaned over her and a wet drop splashed on her face and woke her up but she had the good sense, even so young, to keep quiet and pretend she was asleep.

She could remember what he'd said. It was very simple. 'Bye bye my darling. I'll always love you.'

Liar.

How could he love her from so far away? Never holding her, never hearing her stories?

At first she drew pictures to send him, then when she had learned to write she composed letters and poems and fairy tales. Ruth would always dutifully place them in an envelope to post, but Julie never received a thank you, never even a postcard, and

51

when she was much older she found them all in a box at the back of a cupboard.

'I'm sorry darling.'

That's what Ruth had said when Julie dragged her in and showed her the letters and pictures that told the tale of her childhood.

'He couldn't bear to be reminded of you.'

That was the other thing Ruth said. Julie could not believe her ears.

'I sent the first few but he wrote back telling me to stop. He wanted me to find another Dad for you. He said he couldn't do it any more.'

'Liar!'

'I'm sorry love.' She'd said it again. Hadn't she anything better to say than I'm sorry?

'Why did you keep them? Just so I could find them one day and know about it?'

Ruth stroked her hair.

'You worked so hard... I couldn't just throw them in the bin...'

Julie ducked away from her.

'Well, I'll do it. Give them to me.'

'Wait...'

But Julie had rushed downstairs and fed the papers into the fire, one by one, until she had burned her father completely.

After that she'd never been sure which parent had lied to her the most.

They'd be sorry anyway, when her AIDS-ridden wasted body was fed to the flames in its turn. They'd be able to agonize for the rest of their lives over what they'd done wrong. She was certainly not about to tell them. Instead they could worry until the end of their days about why their single beloved virgin daughter had let herself be screwed by an unknown tattooed boy in an inland town.

Why had she?

Oh, never mind. She'd already been through all that.

Anyway, she reasoned, the chances were that he was probably quite healthy. In fact, maybe instead of a lethal microorganism he had left her a larger remembrance.

She could be pregnant.

After all, she had been having periods for almost four years.

She counted.

Twelve eggs a year for four years added up to forty-eight

52

potential babies, and she had flushed them all down the toilet on soiled sanitary towels. It would be quite understandable if nature had taken the first opportunity it could.

She was able to think about this quite calmly, quite rationally, even with a suppressed sense of excitement. She had better find out when her period was due again.

Her diary was in her bag on the bed. She made to leap out of the chair to get it, then checked herself. She might need to be more careful. Rising gently this time she felt the swelling of her stomach push against her ribs as she reached across the quilt and found the chart Ruth had given her to record her cycle.

It would be two days before the forty-ninth egg declared itself fertilised or not. Well, at least it wasn't long to wait.

She remembered when she had begun to menstruate. It was exciting at first, but she'd soon become irritated by this messy intrusion into her life. Every month swimming was out of the question, and riding her bike became uncomfortable. She tried and tried, but just couldn't get the hang of tampons. It was embarrassing to go to the loo at lunchtime and find a red spot on the back of her skirt and know that people would comment on it all afternoon at school. No matter what she did, she always seemed to make a mess, and the boys who giggled at the thought of bras fell into a hushed silence at the sight of blood.

It was the secrecy which made Julie more angry than anything.

'It's perfectly normal,' the nurse had proclaimed as long ago as the last year of primary school, and the Human Reproduction class in the first year at comprehensive had repeated this assurance.

So why did everyone get so embarrassed about it? Why did female teachers whisper to you in the corridor — 'You've got a stain on your skirt, Julie. Better go and wash it off' — when it was common knowledge that the occasional accident was unavoidable?

Why did chemists wrap up your sanitary towels in enormous paper-bags, trying to be discreet when it was obvious by the shape what the contents were anyway? And what did it matter?

'Half the population have periods,' Ruth always said. 'It's nothing to hide or to be ashamed about.' And Julie had not been ashamed. But it seemed that everyone else was. And because of that, she felt that she would have to be coy about it too.

So not wishing to be thought 'fast' she played the game and soon she was blushing with the rest. But her blushing came half

53

from anger at herself for going along with the stupid pretence that periods never happened, and half from anger at biology for dealing her such a cruel and inconvenient blow.

Once in Liberal Studies they had discussed fox-hunting and the practice of initiating new riders by smearing them with the blood of the dead fox.

Blooding.

That was it, she realised. She had been blooded. She had joined a secret society from which boys were excluded and which they didn't dare to crack jokes about, let alone discuss it seriously.

What's more, periods didn't even feature much in girls' magazines. OK, you could read about them in the problem pages, but they never stained the lives of Wayne and Duane, Mandy and Sandy, the story characters.

Sandy never said 'I've just got to pop to the loo to change my towel', and she and Mandy never discussed the comparative merits of towels and tampons. Sometimes they mentioned Spots, and they often mentioned Fat, but Blood never came into it. The secret society was so secret that even its members kept it taboo from each other.

And then there were secrets within secrets.

Julie made her calculations.

By the time they'd finished dinner the rain had slowed to a gentle shower, and Ruth decided it was time for some fresh air. The brief nap had revived her and she was ready to explore the village. Julie found the idea uninteresting but her mother persuaded her there would be more entertainment in a stroll than in staying cooped up in their small room counting the hours until bedtime.

So they set off.

First stop was the bridge they'd seen from the window. The river still torrented through the village leaving flecks of dirty foam against the banks.

Further on they came to a churchyard and pushed open the heavy gates. As they walked between the gravestones a loud blackbird flew on just ahead, waiting every time they paused then urging them on with its brittle call.

The church was locked but Ruth took her time examining the decoration around the outside until Julie could stand it no more.

'Oh why do you always take so long?' she bleated impatiently, aiming a kick at Eliza Phillips 1813-1864 Rest in Peace.

'Won't be a minute.' Ruth fingered the heavy iron nailheads of the door which would not allow her entry.

But half an hour later she had only progressed halfway round the building, stroking her way like a blind woman who dared not lose contact with the stone.

'Right. That's it.' called Julie. 'I'm going back to the hotel. I've had enough.'

'Just a minute...'

But too late. The heavy gate swung back again and Ruth was left alone to continue reading the ancient braille. Every chisel mark. Every dab of mortar. When she had completed the circuit she sat down on a bench and sniffed the wet air.

Julie had little patience with Ruth's passion for history — and of course, why should she? Ruth had long ago accepted that she couldn't expect other people to like the same things she did. She'd grown used to enjoying her pleasures alone.

When Julie was small her mother had tried to tell her stories about people in the past, but the tales often got entangled in themselves and faded away before they were finished. When you've spent your whole life in study it's hard to refine the facts down to a manageable form, and Ruth had always been a stickler for detail.

However, although she was reconciled to Julie's disinterest, she'd never fully understood it, and could not help but see it as a dismissal of herself. When she was a child she had loved visiting old places and would sit for hours just imagining — something Julie had never done. But then, Ruth had grown up to be a historian, whereas Julie's future was still in the making.

Ruth's job was to untangle the massed threads of knowledge and then to retwist them into a tidier pattern of knots. History is a matter of interpretation, and she had become skilled at transforming the lives of individuals into coherent strands. Inside her head swarmed a multitude, constantly re-telling their stories to each other, and she received a monthly salary to seize a few each week, like an angel plucking up drowned sailors by their golden earrings, and revive them before groups of bored students. They in turn injected dye into the veins to follow the tracks of societal dis-ease, then crumpled the bodies until they were small enough to fit into five thousand words with footnotes. Which Ruth was paid to read and mark before replacing them, bruised, battered, and soiled, back into the controlled environment of her mind.

As the years went by she found it increasingly burdensome to deliver a coherent lecture on anything, and when parading her line of hostages, she frequently became confused. Where once she had everyone clearly sorted and labelled, latterly their identities blended into a monotonous litany of failure, wrong decisions, brutality, naivety... thus history marched on.

So — how good in this country churchyard to confine herself to private, unpaid thoughts. She was under no financial obligation to make an analysis of the skylark soaring above the steeple. Numbers of magpies need not be counted. Worms tunnelled unfettered from one grave to the next, and here the dead did not plead for a new appraisal of their mortal lives.

Liberated by the freedom to be ignorant she raised her closed eyes to the late warmth of the setting sun... and found there...

...many hues.

Rainbows and prisms.

Holograms and blind spots.

Laser beams and silverlinings.

The colours sent the past into slumber as Ruth crossed her fingers and wished for a friend with which to share the serenity of the evening.

This person would be no more than a mirror image of herself, but she found it hard to believe that somewhere in the world there existed another human being who enjoyed the cool stone of churches in exactly the same way that she did.

Is there anyone out there who will climb a hill with Ruth and pause to admire the view at precisely the same moment?

Who enjoys a large breakfast and forgets to eat lunch?

Who likes red and blue?

Who, whenever they spy a gull inland, thinks of Joni Mitchell and her songs of seabirds and sailors?

Is there anyone who likes to sit on a bench in a country churchyard and sniff the wet air because it reminds them of the moss on Irish trees?

Her mind turned to the boat-man.

If it could be someone who looked a little like him — sea-weathered and coarse-featured — but with all of her own remembrance in his mind. Not a facsimile memory, but shared experience. A community of perceptions. A community of two.

He would stroll past the flowering graves and smile inquiringly before sitting down beside her and commenting:

'What a beautiful evening! The air smells just like Irish moss!'
And her eyes would light up with a thrill of recognition.
'Do you know? I was just thinking the very same thing!'
'Isn't it amazing,' he began, 'that the trees in Ireland can be so covered with moss and yet still continue to grow?'
'And the walls too,' she added. 'Although, of course walls don't grow...'
They laughed.
He said 'When I was a kid I used to wait for the rain to stop then I'd go out to hunt for mushrooms. But I never ate any because every single one I picked looked poisonous. In fact, I still wouldn't trust myself to know which ones you can cook...'
'I did that!' she cried. And they laughed again.
She turned to him in amazement. His image was slowly settling and becoming solid until through the strength of her imagination she believed she could even touch him. But she didn't dare.
'Have you been inside?' He asked, walking towards the porch.
'No. It's locked... oh.' He had pulled open the door and was beckoning her to follow. '
That's strange.' she said. But then she remembered that imaginings are powerful things, and she had, after all, worked very hard to conjure him up. She wondered whether to try out the name she had given him.
'Ruari?'
He paused inside the doorway, then turned towards her, his face hidden in the gloom.
'Yes?'
She stared at him in disbelief.
He smiled in the darkness. 'You're thinking it's working. And it is.'
He walked over to the baptismal font and lifted off the heavy carved cover to reveal a cupful of water in the stone basin.
'Come over here.'
He lifted the lid and set it down gently on the paved floor, then dipped his finger into the holy water and brought it to her mouth.
Wordlessly, she tasted.
All the while his eyes fixed on hers and as his finger touched her lips she savoured salt and felt herself sink into the greenness of his eyes.
Still gazing at her, he smiled.
His lips were very red and succulent. Inviting.
She in turn dipped a finger, and with his smooth tongue he

57

received from her a blessing.

'Ruari.'

Now he was sanctified.

Taking a small dust-black book from a nearby shelf he read out softly:

> *I am poured out like water, and all my bones are*
> *out of joint; my heart also in the midst of my body*
> *is even like melting wax...*

Smiling, he carefully replaced the lid of the font and took her arm.

She felt abruptly embarrassed.

'That was sacrilegious. It must have been,' she said uncomfortably.

'Only for mortal people. I don't think we're quite mortal just now, do you?'

'No. I don't suppose we are...'

She looked around at the dark recesses of the building with its lists of the dead hung with dusty banners and suddenly she didn't want to be there any more.

'Let's go outside.'

They left the churchyard by a wicket gate which led straight into a sloping damp field. Below them the village turned on its lights for the evening while Ruth scanned the landscape, past the darkening hills and the moorland and the houses until she came again to Ruari, watching her in the dusk.

There was one broad flat stone in the meadow, big enough for two.

They lay down.

When he kissed her his tongue entered her mouth just a little and their saliva mixed.

Like a river flowing down to the sea she split herself into a thousand running rivulets until his saltiness dissolved within her.

Fish should be touched very carefully. Their scales are covered with a very fine and delicate skin, and rough handling can cause major damage.

Loss of skin is the equivalent of a burn wound in humans, but worse than this perhaps is that the laceration will begin to leak water and salts. Something that may seem like only a minor injury to us can put the fish under great stress as well as providing a site for the spread of infection.

Any dry surface will seem abrasive to the sensitive flesh of the animal so if you must pick up a live fish, make sure your hands are thoroughly wetted first so that you don't cause it any pain.

Later, Ruth lay awake in the darkened hotel room. She was stunned and thrilled by Ruari's materialisation, but barely surprised. After so many lonely years of feeding her imagination with fantasy people it seemed quite natural that at last one of them had come alive. And so perfect! She had only to close her eyes and she could see him, a man come straight from the sea.

Songs are like tattoos, Joni sang. And so are dreams, thought Ruth. Some leave an imprint which cannot be erased and their colours never fade.

Daydreams the same.

She was sometimes afraid of the strength of her daydreams. It was often Ruth's experience to want things so badly that she lost the power to remain in reality. So many imaginary conversations, such intense fantasies of lovemaking with people she had never even touched, that she lived in constant terror of being overtaken by them. An error which could lead to humiliation.

Alex, for example.

When Alex first kissed her it was no real surprise because she had anticipated it so many times already. Snuggling down to sleep she had often turned to the emptiness beside her and whispered goodnight.

But when he attended her lectures through the months preceding that kiss, his presence had sealed her in an invisible and airless chamber from inside which she struggled to speak.

She was trapped in an aquarium of echoes while there he was, breathing a different air beyond the glass.

Out of reach.

From below the surface, she hears the ripples of his voice mingling with those of the other spectators, and she fins nearer until her face almost presses against the thickened pane.

For a moment he catches sight of her bleached eyes and her

silent open mouth, then he turns and moves away with the crowd. She tries to follow him, palming her way along the glass, hands whitened with pressure, but with every call her voice gives out only bubbles.

She cannot understand what he is doing out there. Surely his place is on the other side, her side? The corridor is warm and dark, lit only by the fluorescent strips of the tanks, and the heat has turned his skin a boiled lobster-red. Sweat curves along his pale brow as he glances at each exhibit.

But now Ruari had arrived.

With the sheer force of her longing she had smashed her way through from the real to the unlikely and now they floated together above the shards.

The room that night was thick with the air of new conceptions. While Ruth lay pretending to sleep and thinking daydreams in the dark, Julie tossed and turned in the next narrow bed, gasping for air in a subterranean tankful of babies.

After leaving Ruth to her reveries in the churchyard, she had returned to the hotel and locked the door of the communal bathroom. The air was damp from a recent occupant and smelled of male toiletries. She found the unusual odour rather disgusting. Condensation lay on every cold surface, and she wiped extravagant lengths of pink tissue along the edge of the bath and the seat of the toilet. Meanwhile she breathed shallowly, waiting for her senses to accustom themselves to the perfumes of sweat and masculine cosmetics until she couldn't smell them any more.

She ran the bath hot and deep.

There was a radiant heater fixed high on the wall. Pulling the cord so that soon she felt a glow of warmth on her face, she took off her clothes and, after using more tissue to wipe the mirror of condensation, surveyed her naked body.

These were the breasts he had touched. Trying to imagine how they had felt to him, she ran both palms across until the nipples stiffened at her touch. Below, her belly rounded out plumply so that she could not properly see her pudendum without slightly leaning forward.

She was full of curiosity.

Before, she had been too shy to examine her own body, but now since he had taken the knowledge it seemed reasonable that

60

she, too, should find out.

Curling hedgehog, she opened her labia with fingertips and tried to see, but the more she curved towards it the further her vulva twisted out of view.

On the windowsill she found a small shaving mirror with a cluster of dark stubble clinging to the frame. She wiped it carefully then turned off the rushing hot bath tap.

Then, raising one foot on to the edge of the bath, she lowered the mirror until she could catch a reflection of that part of her so concealed that she could not see it unaided.

This was the first time she had ever dared to look, and she was confused by what she saw.

In the past she had examined anatomical diagrams of female genitalia which made the whole thing seem very straightforward. A row of three entrances leading to tunnels with different uses. But now, although she thought she recognized the tight knot of her anal sphincter — which looked like those of dogs who carry their pink anuses proudly beneath upturned tails — beyond that, she couldn't find any holes at all. She had to fumble along the folds until she found an indentation which might or might not be what she was searching for.

She felt around carefully, afraid of damaging herself with her fingernails.

So gently, gently, she probed and pushed at the dent until suddenly, quickly, one finger slipped into the muscular aperture and it closed around her like a meaty trap. Startled, she pulled her finger out again and examined it. It was dry and unsullied and there was nothing to see.

This wasn't like the inside of your ear, where the folds are smooth and firm, resistant to pressure.

Nor like the interior of a nose, faintly sticky and cartilaginous.

Or the mouth, a wide and mappable cavity.

Although she had never seen an erect penis she had felt its girth in her blind hand, and she could almost imagine it squeezing between those grasping walls, but a baby... it seemed unthinkable that anything so large could pass through.

As a small child she had taken piano lessons. They often began with games. She would stand before the instrument with her eyes closed, turn around three times very fast, then stop and dizzily try to lay her finger on Middle C first time.

This was a similar situation.

Having found her vagina once, would she be able to locate it

61

again? She chose not to describe a magic circle by turning round thrice, but simply closed her eyes and thrust out her hand, pushing out her fingers one by one until she found it. Not perfect, but faster than the first time. On this second occasion it felt more familiar and she kept her finger inside for a little longer, delving around and pressing against the walls. As with the loss of her virginity there was surprisingly little sensation. The only tactile messages came through her fingers, while the blubbery vagina seemed to feel nothing at all. She wondered curiously where the pleasure was supposed to come from.

Slightly giddy with concentration, Julie lowered her leg to the damp linoleum and raised herself upright. As her head cleared she congratulated herself on acquiring all this new information. Holding the shaving mirror under the hand-basin tap she rinsed it with running water, worried that some evidence of her research might remain on the glass, then replaced the dripping mirror on the windowsill and climbed into the bath.

By now the water had cooled considerably but it offered her a relieving embrace. She sunk into its warmth and wondered if her period would come.

Later, in her sleep, she swam with babies in a vast submerged cavern. Phosphorescent microorganisms floated in ripples around a mass of writhing newly-formed limbs. The infants' eyes were all sealed shut like puppies and their cetacean wails echoed plaintively through the water. As their tiny suckering palms clamped onto her arms and legs she struggled to free herself without causing them injury.

Travelling alone with Ruari in a spinning brown coracle, Ruth was startled out of sleep by a single whimper from her daughter's bed. Then they both sank again into their liquid dreams.

Part Two

Bobby Shaftoe's gone to sea
Silver buckles on his knee
He'll come back and marry me
Bonny Bobby Shaftoe

Bobby Shaftoe's tall and fair
Combing back his yellow hair
He's my ain for ever mair
Bonny Bobby Shaftoe

The next morning the sun shone dry and bright as Ruth hummed a sea-song and drew back the curtains. The moorland stream lay glittering below, signalling the urge to move on.

She consulted her guide book, went downstairs to the polished lobby to make a telephone call, then returned to the room and woke up her daughter.

Julie surfaced from sleep and staggered to the bathroom where, stepping into last night's memories, she investigated once more. Still no red. She imagined a stirring inside her and felt strangely optimistic. After a disturbed night she had come through washed clean by dreams and now she felt able to cope with this pregnancy — if that was what it should prove to be.

A boy or a girl?

Yes, she would certainly breast-feed it.

And it would undoubtedly love her. In fact there could be a great many benefits...

At breakfast, she was attracted by Ruth's plan to go west until they could continue no further. Going to extremes in extremity. Well, why not? And her mother had even decided on a little extravagance for once — she had phoned ahead already and booked two single rooms. This was a first. In the past they had always shared, both for the sake of economy and for companionship. Julie wondered briefly what had brought about the change, but decided not to ask any questions. It would be pleasant to have the chance of some privacy for once.

Setting off through the steep hills Ruth sensed an extra presence in the car and, glancing in her mirror, was delighted to see Ruari dozing in the back seat, his feet up on the upholstery. She couldn't resist commenting to Julie about the heavier pull on the steering wheel, although she did not dare to suggest the cause, merely remarking instead on the added weight of the car. Her daughter, map-reading in the front seat, expressed surprise at this strange occurrence whilst inwardly attributing it to her own secret multiplication.

Each smiled a private smile as they drove on gaily, humming to the radio and deep in their own mysteries.

Ruth finally turned off the engine when they reached Portpatrick, western harbour of the Galloway coast. In former times it was the main port for travellers to Ireland, until superseded by the quiet waters of Loch Ryan and Stranraer. Now it lay sleepily quiet with only a few private vessels and a life-boat nestling in its battered arms. Resisted by the waves time and time again, the harbour walls had almost given up the fight, leaving various piers jutting out to sea, ragged and crumbling.

A hundred years before, there had been a phase of rapid expansion here:- an early version of a wave-driven generator; a railway; a loading dock; lime-kilns — but all had been given up. When times got hard and the Isle of Man ferry no longer stopped for passengers, travellers were reduced to waiting in the pub until midnight when they knew the ship would be steaming past. Then they took pieces of smouldering peat from the fire, rowed out into the open sea, and waved the turf in the wind until it burst into flames. At this signal, the passing vessel would stop and take them on board.

These days, dusty shops and a row of pubs still lined the harbour wall, but the travellers came by car and stayed instead in an enormous cream-painted hotel standing in turreted grandeur above cliffs covered in orange montbretia.

Ruth and Julie entered the foyer of the cliff-top hotel with excitement, only to be immediately dismayed by its hushed and murmuring luxury. They were accustomed to cheaper accommodation and, embarrassed by their travel-worn appearance, took sanctuary in their rooms as quickly as they could.

Somehow Ruth had expected Ruari to have arrived ahead of them, to be waiting for her stretched out on the clean-smelling candlewick bedspread, so she was disappointed to find him absent. But then it been no more than an idle fancy. After all, she reminded herself, he was only an apparition.

You shouldn't expect too much.

Still in the memory of his caresses, she entered the cool whiteness of the bathroom and switched on the strip-light above the mirror. Examining her reflection therein, she was pleased. The previous few days on the north east coast had tanned her face, leaving her nose darker and shinier and highlighting the few freckles on her cheeks. Beneath her lower lashes where the flesh was normally blue and tensely drawn, there was now a whitened half-moon, though with her fingers she could still stretch apart the laughter lines beside each eye to reveal a blanched scar where the sun had failed to penetrate.

She liked herself like this, weather beaten and harshened. It made her feel powerful, attractive, erotic, and well-protected. Strong. Invulnerable.

She scrubbed her teeth until they shone white in the mirror, washed her face with a scented cream, smoothed on lotion to retain her tan, and changed into a swimming costume. The full-length mirror made her look rather svelte, she thought. Grinning, she picked up her towel and went to join Julie at the surprisingly empty pool which lay rippling in an ocean of neatly-clipped grass.

Motor boats hummed in the distance as Julie dabbled her toes and Ruth dove straight into the cold blue water. She swum three lengths before she could catch her breath. The sun was hot, the sky cloudless, the hotel garden quiet. They lay in the warmth of the western afternoon, closed their eyes, and kept their thoughts to themselves.

After dinner Julie declared herself too tired for a stroll. She was finding it difficult to accustom herself to the professional nurturing of the hotel, with its well-trained staff and Courtesy tea, Courtesy coffee, Courtesy shampoo, Courtesy mending-kit and Courtesy-God-knew-what-else.

In the dining-room that evening she had been acutely embarrassed by the polite waiters. Awed by their skill of holding a hot dish between two forks whilst serving her, she had allowed them to pile too much food on her plate, and then was shamed by her inability to finish it all. She stared out of the window at the sea and evaded their eyes when they came to remove her still-full plate. And all through the meal she had scrutinised Ruth's table manners, reprimanding her mother in a hushed voice at the slightest fall of a crumb.

She couldn't wait to escape to her room, throw off her shoes, and belch loudly and with relief.

Then she lay down on her bed and began a new chapter in her diary. She had decided to compile a list of possible names. Lily? Rowena? Sparky? Ted? She would draw up two columns and fill them. The irony of the fact that this child, too, would be raised without a father had not yet occurred to her.

So Ruth went down to the harbour alone and settled herself on a sea-ward facing rock with the idea that she would re-memory Ruari. She could taste him, salty on her lips, and beneath her clothes she could feel his white touch on her skin... but soon she was distracted by the water running fast and green below her and out into the Irish Channel.

It was so frustrating, all that life and business going on down

65

there and invisible to her eyes. The dark deeps.

In front of her fluttered miles and miles of tiny white waves. She hoped they were signs of drama — a leaping fish; a dolphin; a shark; a shipwreck.

She had never been able to bear not knowing what was going on.

She cupped her palms to her brow and strained to see. What was happening down there?

Then she reprimanded herself sternly for giving way to such aching curiosity.

The puzzle of the ocean is like the mystery of Ruari, she warned herself.

Don't ask too many questions. Even if she were given the answers she wouldn't be able to understand them.

Don't seek too closely. Don't be so naive. It's a hostile environment out there. She would be unlikely to survive the trip...

A bulky compass jelly fish sashayed into view. Easily a foot across, it was a deep browny-red with creamy frills and many worm-like red tendrils hanging beneath it. As it drifted by alone, it pulsed like a huge gelatinous flower, contracting in regular intervals around its perimeter.

Watching it squeeze along its solitary route, Ruth recalled the free-floating, bumping babies in the clear pools of Longstone.

No-one else seemed to have noticed the creature although by now there were other people wandering along the sea's edge. They were all paired into couples, more interested in each other than in the waters below.

Seeing them holding hands, she was suddenly cut by a sharp spasm of loneliness — quite brief and almost painless this time, but reminding her once again of Ruari and the churchyard. The rain. The pale stones.

On returning to the hotel she knocked on the door of Julie's room but received no response. She must already be fast asleep.

Ruth retired to her own bedroom, once again half-expecting Ruari to be there waiting for her, but still there was no sign of him.

OK.

She'd been a fool.

She climbed into bed, lit a cigarette, and worried about herself. She must really be going crazy to be reduced to imagining such a strange love affair. Only yesterday evening she had honestly believed that she was laying in the arms of some flesh-and-bone lover, a real transubstantiation. Magic. Well, obviously that was rubbish. But if it hadn't happened what, then, could be the explanation? Had it been some sort of fit? Perhaps it was a minor stroke, or the beginnings of a gruesome brain disease. As she hyper-ventilated nervously on nicotine her heart began to race and she was filled with fear for her own body.

That must be it.

She would have to stop smoking.

The hallucination of Ruari had been no more than an ethereal warning from upstairs — Give Up, Or Else.

She stubbed out her cigarette reluctantly, turned out the light, and immediately began to weep.

The next four decades stretched out before her in an endless unlit tunnel of solitude.

Another few years, and Julie would have left home for good. There would be no stopping her. After that — Ruth would continue teaching until retirement, and then... a void. The best she could hope for might be to become a Grandmother.

My God!

Was that how she was destined to fill out her days — babysitting?

Of course, she could escape the perils of being a dumping-ground for Julie's babies if she managed to buy the isolated retirement cottage she had always longed for... but hold on a moment... she was making a lot of assumptions here. Julie might not have children. Maybe she would find a partner but stay childless — many couples did these days. She might choose to love only women, or she could eventually decide to have a baby alone. A lot of women lately seemed to start a family when they reached the age of thirty, whether they had a partner or not. And nothing wrong in that, she mused. In fact, maybe it would be the best idea. The only shadow in Julie's life so far had been Simon's departure and subsequent silence. Perhaps if Ruth had just allowed him to impregnate her then had the baby alone they would all have been saved a huge amount of pain.

The idea of Julie as a thirty-year-old single mother began to appeal to Ruth. They could all live together — and she need never fear being lonely again.

How selfish, to depend upon your only child to fill up the gaps in your life.

Anyway, she decided, she would be getting old by then, and

she'd be much too set in her ways to tolerate disturbed nights and toys all over the place. Sweets stuck to the upholstery. Endless little friends visiting and making mud-pools in her garden.

No thanks.

No thanks, she muttered to herself, dry-eyed now, as she drifted off to sleep.

No thanks. I'll find something else to occupy me for the next forty years.

By breakfast time Julie had begun to relax and enjoy the hotel. She ordered a large plate of scrambled eggs and tomatoes, but Ruth only picked at her food. After a solitary night she had woken up feeling depressed and bad-tempered, and Julie's good mood only irritated her further. The child seemed to think she could get away with changing like the wind, and Ruth was expected to suppress her own caprices and go along with it. Well, Julie might have decided to be good company today, but Ruth had no intention of being other than withdrawn and uncommunicative. Give her a taste of her own medicine.

'So — what was the harbour like?' inquired Julie cheerfully as she buttered yet another piece of toast.

'Alright.'

'See anything interesting?'

'No.'

'Many boats in?' This was hard work.

'A few.' Ruth stared out of the window at the secretive sea and let her coffee go cold.

'Oh, come on Mum! What's the matter? You were really happy yesterday.'

'Hum.'

'So, what shall we do today?'

'Why ask me? You never want to do anything I want to do, so what's the point?'

'OK. Fine.' Julie stuffed the last piece of toast in her mouth and pushed back her chair. 'Do what you like. I'm going back to my room.'

A seagull keened on the grass beside the pool

'Suit yourself.' answered her mother shortly. Julie threw down her napkin and left the dining-room.

Immediately, Ruth felt remorse at her childishness and followed

68

Julie to her room to apologise, but the girl would have none of it. She refused to look at her mother, picked up a magazine, and leafed through it angrily.

'Some holiday.' she muttered between her teeth.

'I'm sorry,' pleaded Ruth. 'I had a bad night.'

'Tough. But there's no need to take it out on me, is there?'

'I'm sorry. I'll try not to.' Ruth tried to sound cheerful. 'So — do you want to walk down to see the boats?'

'No thanks. I'd rather be on my own now, if you don't mind.'

Well, I tried, thought Ruth as she returned to her own room. But she couldn't help feeling a little cheered. Venting her bad mood on her daughter had been unfair, but it had actually relieved her own tension and made her feel quite a lot better. She began to face the day a little more optimistically.

Dressing for her walk, she was taken with admiration at her strong legs. Shorts and walking boots always made her feel fit and healthy even before she left the room, although her legs could do with a shave, she reflected. Tiny prickle hairs rose above a faint map of blue veins, and between them the skin was shiny and lightly tanned. Her calves were inscribed with tiny cracks of dryness, like salt marks on hard sand, their strong fore-shortened curves running down into her booted ankles.

A few firm steps across the carpet, and she was able to reassure herself that she didn't need anyone. Not anyone.

Descending the spiral of broad steps to the harbour with the constant white noise of the sea booming in her ears, the historian took over and she made straight for the old cemetery. (She seemed to spend a lot of time hanging around graveyards, she reflected ruefully.)

The first tombstone she found commemorated a watery death, and of course she knew it would only be the first of many. Foreigners came to Portpatrick on business, or as tourists, or were culled from the sea in bodybags.

Like the Splatt family of the gentle county of Devon, passengers on the Orion steamer on the 18th of June 1850. Many people lost their lives that day, but none so many from one family as Betsy Splatt, aged sixty-eight, and her four daughters Mary Ann, thirty-eight, Elizabeth (sweet Lizzy!), thirty-one, Susanna, twenty-seven, and Anna Maria, twenty-two. Husband and father John was either saved — or he stayed at home. The stone did not give this information, but Ruth was pleased to see that it confirmed that *Their loss will ever be deeply and sincerely regretted by a large circle of friends.*

Ruth could just imagine them, hearty Splatts every one! On board the Orion they would have been the life and soul of the party, gathered around the piano in the second-class saloon, with voices as sweet as linnets. She couldn't even tell if they'd been married, but probably the headstone would say so if they were. No no no! The Splatt girls were much too headstrong and far too educated to be anything other than spinsters in the mid-nineteenth century! They were wealthy business-women every one of them with no time for hanky-panky...

...and they would have made short work of Captain Allen Bursley, the dour commander of the American vessel 'Lion of Boston', drowned less than a mile from land in the early hours of February the first 1835. Tolerant but stern, his swollen face had glared up at the salvage-men as if to ask 'What are you doing away from your posts?' and they'd known straight away that he was the captain. When they found the other bodies they still kept the Captain's separate, and buried him separately too:

> *On the left of this stone are interred the remains of seven of his ship's company who perished with him on that fatal MORNING. Captain B was born on the 10th of May ANNO DOMINI 1800 at Barnstaple in the State of MASSACHUSETTS in which place he has left a wife and infant son.*

What silly ideas! Ruth reprimanded herself for such idle and unprofessional speculation about these poor sailors long dead. The remaining part of the inscription reminded her that somewhere across the seas there would still be descendants of the families who paid for the memorial:

> *The surviving relatives of the deceased are deeply grateful to the humane inhabitants of this place for their kind exertions in recovering these bodies from the deep and depositing them with Christian rites in this Holy spot.*

She had just finished reading about William MacLean who, aged only twenty-eight, had accidentally drowned off Carrickfergus in Ireland and been swept by the currents right across the channel and washed up in Scotland, when she was stopped in her tracks by a noisy whooshing sound.

Fireworks in the middle of the morning? Looking to the sky she spied a tail of white smoke arcing high above the bay before it suddenly exploded with a loud bang. Another flare followed, and immediately everyone was rushing towards the harbour. First-floor windows of bed-and-breakfasts were flung open and heads peered out; games of mini-golf and bowls were abandoned; shops and pubs emptied onto the street, and schoolboys gave up diving from the pier in favour of gathering round the RNLI radio-room.

Ruth ran with the others to the harbour rail.

Lugging their sunshine-hued waterproof suits, half a dozen men were boarding a small dinghy to row across to the life-boat resting at anchor in the deepest part of the bay. The engine was already rumbling into life when a late-comer ran along the quayside, his yellows trailing behind him.

'Go to the end of the pier!' Voices shouted. 'We'll pick you up from there!' The craft made its way rapidly to the appointed place and he threw aboard his kit before jumping onto the deck.

Onlookers clicked their cameras and shouted to their friends as the boat sped out of the harbour and into the open sea. Locals watched it leave with apprehension, tourists with excitement, but no-one seemed to know why the alarm had been raised or where the life-boat was headed.

Curious, she decided it would be a good idea to hang around for a while to see what would happen, so she bought a cup of tea at a nearby cafe and sat down to wait for the return of the life-boat.

From her vantage point on the tiny patio outside the cafe she could see the coast of Ireland shimmering in the distance. The warm breeze tangling her hair had probably come straight from the Emerald Isle, but this thought did not excite her.

In truth, she was disappointed by the west and longed for a cold eastern beach with nothing but fathoms of water between herself and an empty horizon. Memories of Bamburgh with its clean sweep of dunes kept returning unbidden to her mind, and as she studied the harbour swill with its plastic bottles and sodden floating paper bags, she wished she had never come.

It was ironic.

She had been cheated twice, and both times by her own fancifulness. Once by the fiction of Ruari, and then secondly by her own expectations of holiday.

It was not in Ruth's nature to protest until conditions became really unbearable. She preferred to concentrate on the brighter aspects of life, and to this end she had developed a capacity for perpetual semi-consciousness. The consequence of this habit of keeping her senses partially closed down meant that she moved through the world shadowed by a certain tristesse, as if her faculties were constantly picking up a dissatisfaction which she refused to acknowledge.

Generally she would be able to see something finer hidden beyond the human debris on the grey beach, but this time there was only the muddy swell of the water; strands of glutinous seaweed moving with a stomach-churning slithering motion in the low tide; dogshit, and on the street the small pinched faces of the locals.

The last twenty-four hours had been too much. They knotted around her in a confusion of desire and disillusion, and she knew, she just knew, that this place wasn't right.

She had grown used to enduring every tedious academic year with the expectation of a holiday to see her through, and she cherished the vision that one day she would alight in a place she knew to be home.

It would be as if the rest of her life had been mere tourism.

She planned her retirement home. Every passing year added more criteria to her mental list, and she checked off the details everywhere she went:

▶ preferably England (although Scotland might do. Ireland was too far, Wales too hostile)

▶ cheap housing (let's be realistic)

▶ a stretch of quiet beach featuring the following:
      shells
      rock-pools
      crabs
      dunes
      resident dolphin (optional)
      dramatic and terrifying waves in the wintertime

▶ a nearby working harbour (to lift the resort atmosphere and provide a little living tradition)

▶ a distant light-house (must be operational)

▶ lifeboat station

Then followed a list of items which were definitely not acceptable.

These included any type of pollution, but most especially floating faeces and old copies of The Sun; mud-flats; a bored adolescent population spending their time writing graffiti on the public toilets and racing their minis along the seafront; ditto amusement arcades, and definitely no military practise ranges.

Although Galloway had many of the plus ingredients, it also had a few of the minuses. Upon her arrival in Portpatrick the day before, Ruth had been immediately enthraled by the place, but on close inspection it was beginning to disappoint her. Try as she might, she could not rid herself of the knowledge that she was only a tourist here. She did not feel at home, and was acutely aware that her presence added to the community only a superfluous layer, a patina of English money pushing back winter poverty for a few more weeks. The weather was too mild, the landscape too uninteresting, the people too pallid.

And the journey along the Solway Firth had depressed her. Luce Bay — such a beautiful name — was marked in its entirety on the map as a Danger Area where the Air Force preyed on sunken targets and unwitting wild-life. The jagged coast so dramatic on paper turned out to be a toothless estuary fringed by a silty flapping half-hearted sea. And she could not get Sellafield out of her mind — it was out there somewhere, beyond the military ranges.

She was a well-practised voracious tourist, accustomed to soaking in every moment, every landscape, reading the guidebooks thoroughly and tracing their recommended routes. She did want to love this place, but already it was defeating her.

As she shaded her eyes to look for signs of the returning life-boat she hoped viciously for news of a maritime disaster.

For something, anything, to make her feel ALIVE.

Then as if in answer to her thoughts, the gentle green ripples parted and the lifeboat reappeared round the point at the same time as an ambulance drove slowly onto the seafront, blue light flashing lazily.

From everywhere people started running back to the harbour, so Ruth left the pot of weak tea she had been unable to drink and followed until she was positioned amongst the most curious, right at the end of the pier.

A murmur ran through the crowd as the ambulance pushed its way through, coming to a stop only yards from Ruth and her fellow watchers, and the boat slowed to meet it.

On the deck lay a long bundle, cocooned in blankets and

strapped to a canoe-shaped stretcher. As the crew moved around it Ruth caught sight of a mop of wet blonde hair and for a moment her heart lurched — but of course it couldn't be Julie. (In fact at that moment Julie was watching from the hotel garden, high up on the cliffs. She had gone for a walk alone, trying to think, then was distracted by the sight of her mother in the crowd. Now she glared down with disapproval at Ruth's ghoulish curiosity.)

The bundle was lifted up to the pier, the straps unbuckled and the blankets pulled back a little to reveal a slight woman in sneakers, shorts and a pink top. All these were soaking wet, her skin goose-bumped and chilled. She wore a great deal of make-up — thick bright blue eye-shadow and cerise lipstick — all presumably waterproof since the painted face had not smeared during her immersion. As the ambulance men whispered to her reassuringly she opened her eyes for a second and looked without comprehension at the knot of onlookers pressing forward to see. She shivered, gave a deep sigh, and closed her eyes again. They lifted her in to the ambulance and shut the doors.

The show was over, and still no-one knew what had happened. Then someone spoke to one of the life-boat crew and the information was passed around with the speed of a flare.

She'd been dozing in a rubber dinghy in a nearby bay, according to the camp-site owner who'd radioed the crew. He'd shouted to her that she was drifting out to sea, but she'd seemed not to hear him, and by the time he came back from making his call she had become no more than a tiny speck among the waves. The dinghy had disappeared completely. It must have overturned in the swell.

She should never have been out there alone, everyone said.

She must be stupid.

Doesn't she understand the dangers of the tide?

She should never have allowed herself to relax.

Stupid.

Stupid.

Ruth turned away, her mind filled with imagining what it must be like to wake up and find yourself tipped into the cold and frightening sea.

She wondered if she would be able to survive.

Did she have the knowledge to save herself in such a situation?

Would she want to?

Contrary to popular belief, drowning seldom involves being suffocated by water.

In fact, the actual mechanism involves a complex process dependent firstly upon the amount of water absorbed through the membranes of the lungs, and secondly upon whether the water is salt or fresh.

Fresh water is much more lethal.

The lungs need only be filled with fresh water for just a few moments before so much fluid is directly absorbed into the blood that its volume can increase by half as much again. In this event the heart suddenly finds itself unable to cope with the increased pressure, and cardiac failure will result.

Immersion in sea water has a less acute affect since the transfer is much reduced, and this is why there is a far higher recovery rate for casualties retrieved from salt water.

And anyway death by drowning is not always easy to diagnose.

To begin with, the external signs change with temperature and with the length of immersion. Retrieved after a short time in the water, the body may appear normal, although there may be profuse frothing from the mouth and nostrils — these are considered to be the classic signs of drowning. (This proteinaceous froth is not simply water-bubbles, but is composed of oedema fluid from the damaged walls of the lungs.)

Submersion in very cold water will cause the skin to flush a striking bright scarlet — hypothermia victims and bodies submitted to refrigeration can look the same. The skin surface may also become wrinkled and sodden after a few hours in the water, but both that and skin colour are indicators simply of immersion, not drowning.

After the external indicators have been interpreted there is still the ambiguity of the post-mortem findings. Less than half of all bodies recovered from the water show the classic signs of waterlogged lungs and air passages filled with froth, and these so-called 'dry-lung' drownings make it hard to distinguish between actual drowning as opposed to sudden death from cardiac arrest. Weed, silt and sand may be useful indicators if they have penetrated deeply into the lungs, but such foreign matter in the trachea may only be evidence of passive percolation after death. For this reason the diatom test is sometimes used.

This test operates from the simple thesis that the presence of these microscopic algae in distant organs demonstrates that the heart was still beating when immersion occurred. They will have been carried through the alveolar membrane and pumped to other organs such as the bone marrow, kidney and liver. On the other hand, should death occur suddenly in the water, or if the body has been deposited there after death, the circulation will have already ceased and the diatoms will have progressed no further than the lungs.

However, seawater has a fairly consistent content of diatoms whilst they occur more rarely in polluted or fast running streams. Their presence is also seasonally affected, and the air we breathe contains a certain amount, so these facts, along with contamination at post-mortem, makes the diatom test untrustworthy at times.

Some say that drowning is a beautiful death, and although this seems unlikely it is certainly true that many survivors tell of having experienced a strong desire to submit to the waves and allow themselves to be engulfed. This is probably due to exhaustion, but it could also derive from a more atavistic longing — perhaps from a cell-memory of our reputed ancestor homo aquaticus.

Not everyone believes in the existence of homo aquaticus, but whether or not it is true that our species originated in the sea, it cannot be denied that few humans do not exhibit a profoundly primeval response to the oceans which surround us.

That afternoon Ruth and Julie drove to Port Logan, which looked as if it should be on the coast of Scandinavia — or Iceland.

Low white houses gleaming in the sun across a broad and sandy bay.

Ruth parked the car at the north end of the beach and they walked along a narrow track until they reached the Logan Fish Pond.

They were still arguing.

'You're so macabre,' continued Julie. 'You should have seen yourself this morning, standing there staring. I was really ashamed.'

'She didn't know I was looking. I mean, she was barely conscious..'

'That's not the point, though, is it? How would you like to be fished out of the sea and have everyone gather round you being nosy?'

'I wouldn't care,' answered Ruth a little guiltily.

'Anyway,' she went on, 'I like to know about these things. There's nothing wrong with being curious.'

'Ugh — I just find it revolting. What's so interesting about other people's pain?' Julie pulled at the heather growing alongside the path and crushed the purple flowers between her fingers.

Ruth thought for a moment.

Yes, she did feel guilty about her greedy fascination with other people's distress, but that was only because it was socially unacceptable to stare at such things. And why shouldn't she be interested?

'Our world's so anaesthetized,' she answered carefully. 'In days gone by, pain was part of every day life. Butchery, mutilation, disfiguring disease, birth defects... they provided more... variation.'

'Variation!'

'Yes. People might not have understood much about the way their bodies worked, but they knew a lot about the consequences of things going wrong. I mean, these days anyone who doesn't fit into the physical norm is shoved away out of sight. But I'd rather see — I suppose I want to know what it would be like if it happened to me...'

'Well, you'll find out soon enough if you carry on smoking the way you do. Look at you — going on about the clean sea air, and puffing away like a chimney. I'm surprised you can breathe at all. It's disgusting.'

This was Julie's favourite hobby-horse. In truth, she was terrified by her mother's smoking. Convinced that Ruth's addiction might kill her at any time, she felt certain that her mother's blatant disregard for her own future meant that she didn't care about Julie's either. How could she go on committing slow public suicide when she had a child to care for? How could she be so irresponsible?

What's more, she had never once tried to give up. When Julie nagged her she would just laugh uncomfortably — 'I don't have much pleasure in life. At least you can allow me this!' — and light another cigarette. This made her daughter furious with resentment and rejection, and she expressed this terror in sulky anger. Ruth then felt misunderstood and beleaguered — so she lit another to make her feel better. And then another...

The Logan Fish Pond is a natural fish larder, fifteen feet deep, secured inside a tidal pool in the rocks and surrounded by a circular stone wall about ten feet high. There is a paved ledge, smooth and slimy and accessible only at low tide, running around the inside perimeter. A metal grille set low into the wall allows the pool to be laundered by every tide, and in the water swim a captive assortment of cod, coley, pollack and a few conger eels.

Julie and Ruth paid a small entrance fee and were taken by the laird's keeper down the rocky steps and onto the slippery paving.

Generally he fed his charges on fish scraps, he told them, but tourists found these too revolting so instead he offered the visitors a handful of fresh limpets. Ruth took a few. Julie said no thanks.

Half a dozen limpets thrown onto the surface brought the fish streaming to the surface, snapping their wide blubbery mouths greedily.

'You can stroke them if you like,' suggested the keeper. 'No thanks,' muttered Julie again, retreating a little way up the steps, but Ruth crouched down and caressed the spine of a large cod.

She had never before touched a live fish. On supermarket slabs their chilled corpses made them seem alien and unlikeable, but this flesh was smooth, soft, and surprisingly warm.

Slightly nervous of the wide snapping jaws, she continued to massage its plump and satiny back.

'It likes this, doesn't it?'

'Oh, he loves it,' smiled the keeper proudly. 'Soft old bugger.'

'Do you eat them?'

'No. They were originally kept for eating, of course, but nowadays we just wait till they're about five years old then we take them out to sea and let them go.'

'That's good,' she mused. 'And meanwhile they're well-fed and protected. Seems like the ideal life.'

The fish rolled along her fingers, then soundlessly dived and disappeared.

For a moment she thought she caught sight of something much larger at the bottom of the pool. Narrowing her eyes against the surface glare, she saw that it was about the size and shape of a man, but it drifted through the weed like a drowned corpse. Before she could alert the keeper to its presence, the creature flicked its long body and sped into the shadows.

She felt dizzy and sick.

Straightening up slowly, she followed the other two up the steps and onto the path outside.

The tiny house stood right on the rocks. Last year the sea had

78

come up so high that it had crashed over the keeper's cottage, hit the rock-face behind, then bounced back against the front door. Water had poured down the chimney.

'Weren't you scared?' asked Julie, curious in spite of herself.

'Terrified!' grinned the man. Then he added 'While you're here, have a look at this...'

A few yards away was another small building which, he explained, had been a bathing hut for the Laird's lady relatives and their friends. It lay beside another tidal pool, this one only seven feet deep, and had been built over a hundred years before so that the ladies could change their clothes in privacy. There was still even a fireplace inside, although the chimney had been washed away. In last year's storms, he told them, the little hut had lain underwater for two hours while he and his family trembled inside their besieged home next door.

While the keeper chatted on, Julie put on a show of increasing disinterest, her surly manner making Ruth feel acutely uncomfortable and embarrassed. He was just telling them the story of seventeen massive basking sharks he had seen swimming in the bay a few years before — 'They're completely harmless, y'know, but ENORMOUS! Never seen anything like it in all my years...' — when Ruth felt she could stand it no longer. From only a few yards distant Julie was emitting an atmosphere of hostility strong enough to deter the most vicious of sea-monsters, let alone the innocuous basking shark.

She made her excuses and they left, sulking and muttering their way back to the car. Ruth began to wonder whether Julie was just too old now for them to be able to enjoy holidays together any more. They used to have such good times, she mused, and it was sad to think that maybe in the future it would simply no longer be possible. After all, you can't stop your children growing up. The irony of it, of course, is that for every occasion when you've wished they weren't around, after they've left home there will be ten occasions when you wish they were.

She recalled her daughter's moodiness at the inland hotel; her unaccountable tears in the cafe; her sulks in the moorland cemetery. If she hadn't had Ruari to think about, Ruth might have put more effort into finding out what was wrong, but as things stood she had other fish to fry.

The half-seen creature in the Fish Pond had given her a flash of inspiration.

As they drove back to the hotel in antagonistic silence Julie brooded about the possibility of a fishlet swimming at that very moment inside her adolescent uterus, while Ruth refined her idea.

Ruari.

Ever since their love-making — and even before, at Seahouses — she had been subconsciously working on a plan to keep him. She was constantly aware of his ethereal presence floating around her, but his corporeal form was hard to capture.

If only she could create something like the land-bound equivalent of the pool she had just seen, then maybe she could keep him while he grew fat and contented. She would nourish him with her imagination and cherish him with love, keeping him captive for ever.

As long as she needed him — and believed in him — he would always be there.

And it seemed that need was the magic which wrought the spell. The stronger it grew, the sooner he would reappear.

By now it was growing dark, and the lanes were gloomy and unlit. She glanced in her rear-view mirror thinking that surely, by now, he must be back.

But the only reflection she could see was one of utter blackness.

According to Greek myth, the fisherman Glaucus was one of the few people to make the transition from land to sea-dweller.

Legend has it that one day he emptied his catch onto a an area of grassy herbs only to find that the fish were eating the herbs, becoming mysteriously revived, and jumping back into the sea.

Curious, Glaucus tasted the herb but the moment it was between his lips he was overtaken by a desperate longing to enter the water. He ran to the shore and threw himself in, where the Gods welcomed him. They pronounced that all that was mortal in him should be washed away and that after undergoing this sea-change he would be one of them.

Bulfinch's Mythology describes his experience thus:

'A hundred rivers poured their waters over him. Then he lost all sense of his former nature and all consciousness. When he recovered, he found himself changed in form and mind.'

The poet Keats tried to imagine how this would feel:

I plunged for life or death. To interknit
One's senses with so dense a breathing stuff
Might seem a work of pain, so not enough
Can I admire how crystal-smooth it felt,
And buoyant round my limbs. At first I dwelt
Whole days and days in sheer astonishment;
Forgetful utterly of self-intent,
Moving but with the mighty ebb and flow.
Then like a new-fledged bird that first doth show
His spreaded feathers to the morrow chill,
I tried in fear the pinions of my will.
'Twas freedom! and at once I visited
The ceaseless wonders of this ocean-bed.

Today Glaucus and his wondrous experience are almost forgotten, yet we still remember him in the dark blue tints of the sea when the wind begins to rise.

Ruth and Julie took their evening meal without conversation.

There seemed to be no way to retrieve the amicable atmosphere which had always characterised their holidays until now. Their minds were taken up with themselves, and neither could reveal her preoccupations. Julie waded in uncertainty, cut off from her mother by the tide of her private experience whilst Ruth yearned only to dream again like Caliban on her private isle of sounds and sweet airs.

As soon as dessert was over they said a curt goodnight and returned in relief to their separate rooms.

Glad to be alone, Ruth stripped off and went to the bathroom to wash. In the mirror she caught sight of herself and was horrified at the extent to which she'd caught the sun that day. Now she had the shiny red complexion of a demented clown, a scarlet nose glowing with heat and already fringed with shreds of peeled white skin. Below the vivid face shone the semi-circle of her chest, burned bright pink from neck to breast-bone. The skin was already bubbling up with tiny blistery spots.

She reached up to brush away a wisp of hair, but as she did so the nail of her smallest finger scratched against a reddened breast, making her catch her breath in pain. Wincing, she threw cold water over the wound and tried to look again.

Her face, thighs, chest, and the tops of her arms were a mess of burns and peeling skin. Suddenly the pain streaked down to her bowels and she rushed to the toilet just in time to expel a violent stream of diarrhoea.

Holidays.

What a disaster.

After a couple of minutes beneath the shower, she staggered to bed in despair. Almost every part of her body was scorched and sensitive.

Then, when she had almost given him up, Ruari reached out from within the deep white pillows and caressed her.

At last it was working again.

She held her breath, fearing the soreness of any touch, however ghostly, on her seared skin. But his fingers were cool, smooth, and inflicted no pain.

He spread his palms and laid them flat against her upper chest, taking the heat away from her and into his own body. Then she closed her eyes gratefully as he began to lick her like a dog, in long slow strokes from throat to breasts and back again, up and down along her wounded flesh, and his saliva made a soothing unction against the burns.

She sighed with relief.

He's back.

She has made him come back.

And, she thought with satisfaction, with an imagination like mine, who needs reality?

By the time he reached the scarlet semi-circles on her shoulders she was cool again. The tight red skin and stinging burns had disappeared as if by magic.

Remembering Port Logan, she began to stroke the damp flesh of his shoulders then, stretching out her arms, she fished him up for a kiss.

What a poor contemptible being is the naked savage, standing on the beach of the ocean, and trembling at its tumults! How little capable is he of converting its terrors into benefits; or of saying, behold an element made wholly for my enjoyment! He considers it as an angry deity, and pays it the homage of submission.

But it is very different when he has exercised his mental

powers; when he has learned to find his own superiority, and to make it subservient to his commands. It is then that his dignity begins to appear, and that the true Deity is justly praised for having been mindful of man: for having given him the earth for his habitation, and the sea for an inheritance.

Oliver Goldsmith
'A HISTORY OF THE EARTH AND ITS ANIMATED NATURE' 1774

In the morning she left Ruari safely asleep in the white-sheeted bed and went to meet Julie for breakfast. She couldn't wait to get home. Ideas were hatching in her mind like frog-spawn, and wriggling with promise.

By ten o'clock they were packed and gone. Once they were safely on the road again, Ruth tried out her plan. She felt cheerful, and in control of her own destiny. She was unaware that her only daughter had also begun to make secret preparations.

'I've been thinking,' began Ruth, 'We don't have to live in the town if we don't want to. We could move! We could go and live in the country!'

Julie sat bolt upright in horror.

'You're kidding!'

'Why not? There's nothing to stop us.'

Julie put on her best teenage scowl.

'Mum, for God's sake! All my friends live in the town. And anyway, there's nothing to do in the country. It's boring.'

Ruth smiled at her indulgently.

'Don't worry, there's no rush. It's just an idea.'

'I bloody well hope so. Anyway, can't you wait a bit? I'll have left home soon, then you can do what you want.'

'Leave home? Why ever would you do that? You've got three more years before you go to university.'

'I'm not going to university.'

'Don't be silly.' Ruth jerked the wheel of the speeding car away from the kerb. 'Of course you are!'

'I don't need to. Most of my friends are leaving after their GCSE's.'

'Oh yes? Like who, for example?' Ruth suddenly realised that she'd hardly ever met any of Julie's friends.

'Dawn, for one. She's going to be a hairdresser.'

Ruth sighed.

'Oh Julie, you can do better than that...'

'I said Dawn is, not me. I've got other ideas.'

'Like what?'

'Well, I might go abroad. Maybe America. I could work in a hotel.' She became enthusiastic. 'I could be a chambermaid...'

'I don't think cleaning hotel rooms makes for much of a career.'

'What do you know? You've never done it!'

You've never done anything, Julie thought. You've hardly stepped outside your own front door.

'But, darling, you're a bright girl. You're doing so well at school, you don't want to waste your abilities. Get some qualifications and then you can do what you like...'

'You don't need a degree to be a chambermaid.'

'Don't be ridiculous.'

'Mum, I'm not being ridiculous. It's time you got used to the idea that things aren't always going to be the way you want them to be.'

Julie was resigning from the family game. She could do what ever she wanted. After all, she reminded herself, she was a woman now.

Ruth took one hand off the wheel to fumble for a cigarette. Lighting it, she inhaled deeply and kept her eyes on the road. All children went through this, she thought to herself. The best idea would be to keep quiet until it had all blown over. Instead she thought about Ruari while Julie gazed out of the window at the rolling Pennines and made her career plans.

Ruth had only ever had two options in her head — staying in the tiny house in town or moving to the sea. Strangely enough she had never considered a compromise, but now that she had Ruari, fresh vistas were opening up before her very eyes.

She knew he would not fit into the life of a town. Of course, he belonged to the sea, but despite her own love for the wide ocean she felt it would be more circumspect to keep him land-locked.

She could, however, consider a river. She could easily imagine him by a river. He would feel reasonably at home yet not so much that he might be tempted to wander.

As they neared home she conjured pictures in her mind of a cosy house with a few fruit trees. Apples, plums, pears, maybe a peach if she was lucky. And hens! She'd always wanted to keep hens. There must be somewhere, she reflected, which lay within commuting distance of the university. There must be a house on a hill with a river winding down below. She could bake bread. Go black-berrying. She could make love to Ruari in the woods at midnight.

Suddenly she heard his soft voice as he leaned forward from the back seat.

'Sounds like a good idea,' he whispered. His breath was moist on her neck. 'Let's do it!'

She grinned.

Yes!

As soon as she got home she would visit the estate agents.

She somehow felt stronger now. After all, Julie was still only a child and she'd soon get used to the idea of moving house. She could make new friends. Get some fresh air into her lungs.

Knowing that Ruari was watching, she smiled.

'Yes! Let's do it!' she exclaimed joyfully.

'Do what?' asked Julie.

'Oh, nothing.'

'Do you realise you've started talking to yourself?'

'Have I?' Ruth chuckled.

'Yes you have. Even in public. I wish you'd stop it, it's really embarrassing.'

'I'll try.' replied her mother happily. 'Hey, by the way,' she added. 'I've had another idea. If we move to the country we might be able to get you a little car in a year or two, then you could take your test and drive to school.'

'I've told you! I won't be at school then.'

'Oh, Julie.' Irritated.

'Look Mum, can't you understand that I'm grown up now?'

'You're not grown up. You're only fifteen.'

'I'll be sixteen in November. Old enough to get married if I want to.'

'Not without my permission. And anyway, who would you marry?'

'No-one. That's not the point.'

'So what is the point, then?'

Julie fixed her gaze straight ahead and clenched her teeth.

'The point is, Mother, that I'm a woman now and I can do what I want.'

But even as she spoke, Julie felt a familiar tightening across her lower stomach, and the recognition brought with it a sudden

85

rush of disappointment followed rapidly by the sense of a different liberation. She turned to Ruth and changed the subject abruptly.

'Can we stop at a toilet? I think I might've started my period.'

Unless she was mistaken, there could not be a baby now. An enormous sense of relief flooded through her, followed by a hardening crystal of conviction.

Over the last few days she had imagined so many different scenarios, yet of them all the most pressing was the idea that if she had a baby she would not have go to university. And it was only when she realised that fact that she knew she had never wanted to go in the first place.

Julie had lived with academia all her life. Books and papers and typewriters. Talk but no action. Ruth had no idea of what the real world was like, the hustle of business and production lines and real money. Her idea of fulfilling employment went no further than the interpretation of a new piece of historical evidence.

What sort of a life is that? asked Julie to herself.

She wanted to be up and doing. A free spirit. She wanted to meet all sorts of people, not just boring academics. People who didn't worry about careers and all that crap. People who made every minute count.

When she came out of the lavatory at the next service station she felt wholly exonerated. The red stain on her underwear had shown that from now on she had the world at her fingertips.

No baby = endless possibilities.

But she would have to be sensible. No more slip-ups.

She would do things properly. Finish her last year at school, get her GCSE's, then hit the road. As far as her mother was concerned — well, let her move to the country. Julie wouldn't be around to have to live there. But there was no point in inviting trouble. She decided to bide her time until next summer.

Returning to the car she said 'I've been thinking. Why don't you look for a new house next year, after I've finished my exams?'

'Good idea.' agreed Ruth, pleased that this quarrel at least seemed to be over. 'We'll do just that.'

Part Three

CALIBAN: *Be not afeard; the isle is full of noises,*
              Sounds, and sweet airs, that give delight and hurt not.
              Sometimes a thousand twangling instruments
              Will hum about mine ears; and sometime voices
              That, if I then had waked after a long sleep,
              Will make me sleep again; and then, in dreaming,
              The clouds methought would open, and show riches
              Ready to drop upon me, that when I waked
              I cried to dream again.

Ruth awakes to a terrible crashing noise and the distant sound of sirens. She staggers to the bedroom window and looks out to find water everywhere.

Water.

As far as the eye can see.

It's too early yet to think of rescue, so she rolls up some newspapers to make a fire.

She twists the paper into sticks, then covers them with coal from the scuttle. But the rain pours down the chimney, putting out the flames before they can take hold.

Bloody hell.

She goes to the kitchen to find something flammable. Meths will do. She pours a little of the unearthly purple water onto the coals then allows a moment for it to soak in before a touch of a match brings the fire alive again.

As she gazes into the new flames a scrabbling at the door has her leaping to her feet to let in a dripping cocker spaniel.

Sophie was the first accessory Ruth had bought for the new house because you can't live in the country without a dog. Chilled and shivering, she now stands obediently waiting to be cared for until Ruth takes an old towel and hustles her to the hearth for a rubdown. They snuggle together before the sparks. There's nothing like an open fire for cheering you up.

Ruari, too, likes to watch the blue gases rise between the glowing coals while she contemplates the red of the flames lighting up the gingery glint of his curls.

Now there is nothing to be done until the river subsides. No electricity, no tv, no radio, no music, no lamps. In fact, it might be a good idea to look for candles.

Outside, the garden is bathed in a dull half-light. It could be the whimpering end of the world.

She finds some dirty white candles in a drawer, and sets about collecting saucers to stand them on. She places one on the table; two on the piano; one on top of the now redundant music centre; two on the mantelpiece. As she touches a match to each one it echoes the fire until the room is filled with brightness. Her shadow moves between the yellow lights. And still the rain sputters against the glass beyond this comfortable retreat while Sophie's damp warm spaniel smell mingles with the perfume of wax, imparting a medieval richness to the stuffy air.

The water continues to rise.

And Ruth tends her gentle fires, unaware that below the vegetable garden the hen-run is already under water.

Inside, huddled on a crowded perch, is a flock of Welsummers. They each have the strong red comb and rich chestnut plumage of their breed, but some move fast and some move slowly. One has a twisted foot. Another drags a wing. They all lay large rich brown eggs every other day.

Now the proud red combs drip water over their jewel eyes. When Ruth let them out this morning they had rushed into the muddy run to scratch drowning worms from the soil, but as the water rose they made their way back up the slatted ramp and into the dryness of the poultry shed.

Very soon the flood followed them in and they had to scramble higher still. With abrupt flutters they regained their perches and pretended that night had fallen too soon.

The hollow at the bottom of the garden fills up quickly and silently. By eleven o'clock only the upper wires of the run can be seen, whilst inside the hen-house gentle waves lift this morning's eggs from the nest-boxes and lower them to the floor. Straw and feathers swirl waist-high, and just above the floating debris ten bedraggled fowls perch and doze, waiting for morning to return.

They shuffle sleepily around in the darkness until one of them slips off into the murky water.

Squawking and screaming, she flaps her wings and tries to fly back up while the others awake to watch her struggle dispassionately.

Somehow her frantic movements bring her close to the door, but the current carries her back inside, and Ruth arrives just in time to see the drowning hen flop its head below the floating straw for the last time.

Sitting curled up by the fire she had suddenly remembered them. Oh Jesus! Oh my God! How could she have forgotten the hens? When she opened the back door she could see only the top of their house above the water, and she had not stopped for coat or boots.

Running, slipping down the slope, skidding on cabbages and

parsnip tops she races towards her flock.

The gate to the run sticks for a moment then gives — its wire construction makes it light in the water. She wades waist-deep into the house. Eggs float against her ankles in the swell created by her movements, and she cannot help crushing them beneath her bare toes.

The first bird is drowned, its chill eyes even colder in death, and with Ruth's entrance the flock begin to panic. They fly up to the top of the roof and then fall back into the flood while she clutches at their flailing limbs, grabbing them in a fist until she has two in each hand. Their scaly legs are slippery between her fingers, and they flap their wings heavily in an attempt to free themselves from her grasp.

Then only three remain on the perch.

They set up a chorus of monotonous shrieks which they repeat in shrill syncopation. Locked into hysteria, there is every chance that they'll stay up there a little longer, so she decides to risk carrying the four flapping birds to higher ground. Leaving two more still swimming for their lives she wades out to dump the four on the sloping path, then fights her way back towards the others.

Her eyes are stinging with rain as she grabs the wing of a floating hen and pulls it towards her. It flaps weakly, vomits into the dirty water, then its body relaxes against her pull.

Two dead.

Collecting the remaining swimmer and the trio of crying birds, she wades out for the last time to see Sophie herding the first four up towards the house. Running to the front of the procession, she leads them through the open door and into the sitting-room. Now at last she can release her hold and drops them heavily on to the carpet, still locked into their manic squawking.

When she goes back to slam the outside door she is suddenly overcome with fury. Standing like Alice in the pool of tears around her feet she sobs. Two dead, and all for this damned rain. She should not leave the bodies outside, but she has no energy left. She is soaked to the skin and freezing cold.

Stripping off her clothes she drops them in a pile onto the tiled kitchen floor.

And the rain pours down.

Inside the house a naked shivering woman stands weeping. A dog and eight bedraggled chickens huddle before the crackling fire.

Now it is nearly noon, and rescue still has not arrived.

She sits by the hearth, dressed once more in soft trousers and a warm jumper. Her flock have for the most part calmed down and only the hen with the twisted foot continues to bleat its panic. Ruth leans over to pick it up and enfolds it in her arms. As she murmurs soothingly into its neck she remembers she has done this before. Six months ago a fox got into the run, killing two birds before Sophie's barking scared it away. That time too, the hens had set up this same monotonous squawk and would not stop until Ruth had cuddled them, one by one, into silence.

The bird is warm and heavy against her breasts. She can feel its thundering heart as she strokes its cool outer plumage, lulling it until gradually it ceases its struggle and quiets down. When it is calm she gently lowers it to the rug and returns her gaze to the fire.

Maybe it's foolish to sit and wait for rescue. Perhaps this time the flood is really serious — perhaps her life is in danger. She resists the urge to take one more look out of the window in case the news is bad. And anyway, what else can she do but sit here? The house is cut off from all sides and there's no question of escape. Still, she can't believe she'll be marooned for any longer than a few hours. She should take advantage of the respite from routine, and simply wait.

Ruari comes in with a tray of tea and food. Bread and cheese and cake. He makes a good cup of tea.

She smiles up at his back as he busies himself with plates and knives, and discovers she is famished.

'My love, you think of everything!' she exclaims as she tucks into a slab of brown bread.

'I know.' He grins, then waves a hand at the hens, who have made a sudden recovery and are now busily scavenging for crumbs around his feet.

'What are you going to do about them? They'll make a real mess in here.'

'I don't mind.' She feeds Sophie a crust. 'It won't take long to clear up. At least they're warm and dry.'

She curls up on the rug and munches contentedly.

Chuck chuck chuck.

He holds out morsels of bread on the flat of his palm and the hens help themselves.

Chuck chuck chuck.

The wind whips up, slashing the rain against the windows and pushing it through cracks in the putty. It dribbles its way inside.

She finishes her food, giving the last piece of cheese to the dog. Now she is restless. She tries the phone again, but it's still dead. Puffing on a cigarette, she wanders round the room trying the light switch, the radio, the electric typewriter. Nothing works. Then she goes to the back door and opens it. The wind blasts into the house and she has no time to look out before it slams shut again. For a moment she had not been able to breathe, her lungs filled by the cold wind.

Things don't look too good. She takes her bird-watching binoculars upstairs to her bedroom window, and once again she cannot believe her eyes.

The nearest house is further down the hill, but the owners are away and have left it locked up. By now its lower windows have disappeared beneath the waters, and furthermore, it has found a mate. Nestled up against the house is a blue caravan, bobbing in the waves. It is a small caravan, of old-fashioned design, and it certainly was not there before. It tips and turns, but manages to remain upright in the swirling torrent because it is jammed between a poplar tree and the twisted framework of a newly-built sun-lounge. Not so sunny now.

In the distance Ruth can just make out the whale-like shape of a single-decker bus swimming down-stream. The water has penetrated its circuits, turning on its headlights. They gleam ghostly as the vehicle rises in and out of the waves.

The view from her house has become somewhat repetitious. The water is grey, the sky is grey. It's hard to tell where one ends and the other begins. The church spire is still identifiable, but the rest of the scene has been reduced to a cluster of roofs. She can still see the tops of the older trees, but the autumn fields are completely submerged.

At this distance, and using her binoculars, she can just make out the movement of tiny boats in the village as they row from bedroom to bedroom. She thinks she can see doll-like figures in upstairs windows, but she cannot be sure.

She puts down the binoculars and looks to see how much of her own land has been swamped. The chicken-house has disappeared altogether, and there is no sign of the dead hens. Some of the vegetables are under water, but due to the steep rise it stands on the house is still surrounded by twenty yards of land on every side. The garden is fringed with debris of all kinds — wood, slabs of polystyrene, paper, small dead animals, clothing, items of furniture, some still unbroken.

But the merman garden ornament, which she had transported so carefully from the pond at the last house, still stands upright by the back door where it seems the ivy has stretched out an arm to bind him intimately amongst its glossy leaves.

The previous year, just after her eighteenth birthday, Julie received a very official-looking letter. The hotel porter handed it to her when she passed through the foyer after work, her legs aching from a long day's vacuuming and bed-making.

Pushing the letter into her overall pocket she climbed the backstairs to the tiny room she now called home. As soon as she opened the door her nose collided with the stench of feet and perfume which built up during the day in the airless atmosphere of every staff bedroom in the hotel. Well, she sighed, the room might be stuffy but at least it was never cold.

By now most girls would have given up trying to make a go of it and run home to mother, she thought bitterly, but chance would be a fine thing. Most of them no doubt had a nice home to go back to, with two respectable parents and a proper house with ruched flowery curtains from M&S and a set of Chambers encyclopedias.

And what did Julie have? A single parent living on a hill in the middle of nowhere, so busy talking to herself all day that she hardly ever cooked a proper meal, and with the scruffiest and wildest hair of any bag-lady in London. She was a pain and an embarrassment, and the birthday card and cheque Julie had received the day before yesterday went no way to making up for it. No distance at all.

There were still lodged in her mind many transgressions for which she could not forgive her mother, but the most serious was the way that Ruth had neglected to help her through those few days, nearly three years ago now, when she'd thought she might be pregnant. Of course, she'd never actually told Ruth about it, but that wasn't the point. A proper mother would have guessed anyway.

And it was also around that time that Ruth had started to become increasingly distracted. One moment she seemed to be going crazy in the head — as if she were hearing voices — then the next she moved about in a state of manic cheerfulness as she put their cosy little home up for sale and began to search for some sort of dream-house. She knew exactly what she was looking for, she said. It was just a question of finding it. She didn't ask Julie what she might have wanted.

It was then, too, that Julie's resolve to leave school had begun to diminish. The results of her mid-term exams had been pretty good, and she'd begun to wonder whether she should perhaps stay on in the sixth form after all. She waited to be persuaded.

But, unusually, Ruth had made no attempt to influence her daughter. It almost seemed as if she rather liked the idea of moving into her new home alone. Already their lives were growing more and more distant from each other, and Ruth spent much of her time closed away in her bedroom. Reading, she said. But she never used to shut herself in just to read.

Sometimes Julie stood in the hall-way and listened to her mother chatting to herself behind the door. Once, woken by voices in the middle of the night, her sleepy mind told her that she'd got it all wrong — that Dad was still there — that he'd never left — it had all been an awful nightmare — and she rushed into Ruth's room only to find her mother lying stretched out naked, alone on the bed with her eyes closed, her fingers between her legs, smiling blindly at the ceiling and moaning unintelligible phrases. Unnoticed and dismayed, Julie turned away and went back to her own room.

Furious and lonely, she started to become more vociferous, constantly button-holing Ruth to discuss her plans to leave home, but still she met with no resistance.

'Fine,' Ruth would answer distractedly, 'whatever you think best.' Often her gaze seemed to be focused on a place above and behind Julie's head.

Time and again she left herself open to be rescued from her own resolve, but Ruth failed to stretch out a hand.

So she gave up.

Without waiting for the results of her summer exams, she took a bus to London and found herself a live-in job. If you can call it living, in this poky stuffy little den. And there she waited for her mother to fetch her away and bring her to her senses. The work was hard and dirty and as she laboured at cleaning yet another toilet bowl she had fantasies of Ruth bursting into the quiet foyer of the hotel and causing a scene. Demanding to have her daughter back.

And she would bury herself in her mother's arms and return meekly to the haven of home.

In her letters Julie always maintained that life in London was great, crossing her fingers in the hope that her mother would read between the lines and see through her bravado. But Ruth's replies were vacant and distracted, so there was nothing to be done but stick stubbornly to her plan. A year later she was still waiting to be rescued, until finally it dawned on her that it just wasn't going to happen. To confirm the truth of this in her mind, she took a few day's leave and travelled north to her mother's hill-top retreat.

It had been good at first. Ruth made a fuss of her and cooked an enormous meal in celebration. She'd obviously worked hard to clean up, and the whole house looked spotless to Julie's now professional eye. But when her mother laid the table, she set three places.

'Mum? What are you doing? There's only two of us...'

'Well, I thought it would be nice if... no, never mind... I'll take one away.'

'Just a minute. What are you talking about? Is someone else coming?'

'No, no, it's okay. Really. Forget it.' And she quickly put away the extra plate, glass, and cutlery. But the three table-settings had started off another train of thought in Julie's mind.

'Have you heard from Dad recently?' she inquired innocently, knowing very well what the answer would be.

Ruth stared. 'Now what ever makes you think I might have done? I haven't heard a word from him for years. You know that.'

'Oh, I just wondered. You know...'

With a start, Ruth realised that her daughter was almost a grown woman. No doubt she had boyfriends. And in that light of course it made sense that she'd begin to be curious about Simon.

'Would you like to get in touch with him?'

'I thought you didn't know where he was.'

'I don't. But presumably my bank does, because he still pays the maintenance. I told you I've been putting it into a savings account for you ever since you went to London.'

'I'd forgotten about that!'

Julie filled up their wine glasses with relish. This was great. All of a sudden she had money in the bank; Ruth was being reasonably sane (except for the episode with the table settings, but she quickly brushed that aside), and this old ramshackle house was even beginning to feel like home.

'Anyway, you could probably contact him through my bank if

you wanted to.'

'Hum.' Now that there was a real prospect of seeing Simon, Julie wasn't so sure if she did want to. 'I'll think about it. Did you grow these potatoes yourself? They're gorgeous...'

They had spent a pleasant evening together, but in the middle of the night everything was spoiled again.

At four a.m. Julie was woken by an insistent beat running through her sleep. Rubbing her eyes she realised she wasn't dreaming — there really was a blues party going on downstairs. What on earth...?

In the sitting-room Ruth was dancing to a pounding reggae beat. Get up, stand up. Stand up for your rights...

'Come on, Ruari!' she cried, 'You can't be tired out already! No, that's no excuse. I won't accept it...!'

Julie stood at the door in her night-gown with an awful feeling of having been here before.

'What's going on?'

'Oh, tell him for me Julie. He says he can't dance any more! He's just a lazy old...'

'But... there's nobody there.' Julie switched off the music and ripped out the tape. 'Mum! There's no-one there, for God's Sake!'

What the hell was she supposed to do in this situation? She couldn't cope with a crazy mother. After all, she was only a kid. Tears flushed into her eyes and she sank onto the floor in despair, Ruth's spaniel crowding round her sympathetically.

'What's the matter with you?' she shouted. 'You really are cracking up, aren't you? Is this your imaginary boyfriend again? Is it? Come on, tell me...'

'He's not imaginary,' replied Ruth calmly, 'He's real. He's just not quite the same sort of real that you're used to... oh, don't cry...'

'Get away from me! You're nuts!' She jumped out of her mother's embrace and rubbed her hands furiously through her cropped hair in a long-lost gesture from childhood.

'I'll make us some tea.' The older woman took a cardigan from the back of a chair and wrapped it around her shoulders before entering the chilly late night kitchen. While the kettle boiled she stirred up the fire and brought it back to life, then they sat silently, mug in hand, watching the flames.

Julie, calmer now, tried to explain.

'Look, Mum, I'm sorry. I don't really think you're crazy, but I do think you're very lonely. You ought to get out and about more. There must be plenty of men you could go out with, even if it's just for... you know... a bit of comfort. I worry about you on your own.'

'That's sweet of you, love. But you don't have to. I know it's hard to believe, but I'm quite content. And I'm not at all lonely because I've got...'

'Don't. Don't say it.'

A snapshot stood framed upon the mantlepiece - the pair of them on some beach somewhere sometime, both in cowboy hats, both grinning like fools. Julie picked it up.

'I love this picture. It always makes me laugh. I must have been about — what? — eight?'

'Nine, actually. Oh yes, there's nothing like a family photo for bringing back good times,' smiled Ruth.

'The trouble is that we've never been a real family, have we? Isn't that the problem?'

'Oh, I don't know if I'd say that. Good God, there are certainly plenty of single-parent families around these days. It's almost de rigueur!'

'Well, I'm sorry, but I don't think it's right. I mean, look at you. You spent the best years of your life — I know it's a cliche, but it's true — the best years of your life working every day then staying in at night to look after me. And who looked after you? No-one. That should have been Dad's job.'

'That's rather out-of-date isn't it? I'm surprised at you, Julie!'

'Oh, I don't mean that he should have looked after you in an old-fashioned, chauvinistic sort of way. I just mean that everyone needs someone to love them.'

Ruth pulled a face. 'Don't remind me! Your grandmother used to say that all the time.'

'Well, she was right. I mean, it was all very well for Dad just to bugger off when he had another woman waiting in the wings. But you, Mum, you've been so alone. All these years...'

'Well, that's just the way it is,' Ruth answered soothingly. 'You have to be philosophical about it.'

'Well, I'm not! As far as I'm concerned, he's a bastard!' She was shouting now. 'He doesn't deserve any love at all. He's a total shit!'

'But,' replied Ruth calmly, 'you still want to see him.'

'Perhaps. But I don't know what I'd do. Kick him in the balls, probably.'

'Come on, it's nearly dawn. Let's get some sleep. There's no point in crying over spilt milk.' Good old Ruth, she had a platitude for every occasion.

She had put an arm around her daughter, taken her upstairs and tucked her into bed. It was almost like old times.

But in the morning Ruari was back. She heard Ruth talking to him downstairs in a low voice so that Julie wouldn't hear. That afternoon she caught the next train back to London, and vowed that from then on she would stay away. It hurt too much. Ironically, that's just the way her father would have seen it too.

Sometimes a river meanders in a sharp loop then returns to its original course leaving a bite-shaped area of land within the curve which we call an oxbow. But the rapid sweep of the river can cause the banks to be so quickly eroded that before long a new section of silt has arisen and the river is redirected once more back onto a straighter flow.

The product of all this rearrangement is often an oxbow lake left in the depression caused by the stray meander, and it was such a lake which lay at the bottom of the hill where Ruth lived with her transubstantial lover. It was here that they reaffirmed the betrothal pledged in the moorland church, and here that they made their truest wedding.

Until then Ruth, earthbound, had perceived the lake as no more than a horizontal interruption in the terrestrial world, but for Ruari it was instantly recognizable as an enslaved fragment of shallow ocean, less turbulent than the river and less expansive than the sea.

It was his place.

The first time Ruth took him there he had immediately thrown off his clothes in his longing to feel the smooth silt beneath his bare feet. Then he silently undressed his lover and led her down the bank. It was a warm day, though perhaps not warm enough for this sort of activity. But she could not resist the strange focus of his eyes so she followed him into the borders of the lake until the water reached the tops of her legs.

Then he stopped, turned, and slowly crouched down in front of her until he was almost submerged. Unconsciously she opened her thighs before him, balanced her feet firmly on the slippery stones below, and watched through half-closed eyes. She was waiting to feel his smooth tongue.

But instead he did no more than gently open her with his fingers and allow the lake to lap at the sensitive flesh.

97

Water is itself almost a sensory organ. It responds to the most minute encounter, and as it re-formed around their bodies it changed and shifted into a flow of tiny ripples which licked against Ruth's clitoris and entered her exposed vulva. Gently, he opened her still wider until she could feel the lake rising up inside her and she held her breath as the tiny waves ebbed and flowed.

Ruari stood back so that only the tips of his fingers were touching her and pursed his lips to blow on the surface of the water, creating even stronger pulses of the most delicate sensations.

Then, as in her desire she reached towards him, he rose up for a kiss, pressing their naked bodies tightly together until the lake retreated and there was only moisture between them.

He put his hands on her shoulders.

Then suddenly he entered her quickly whilst at the same moment pushing her down hard, down under the water, until she was fully submerged.

The lake was above her, filling her ears and nose and mouth, and Ruari filled her sex.

Shocked, she panicked and struggled to breathe, but when she opened her eyes and saw him there before her at home in his true element, the fear went away. She relaxed and held her breath, fascinated and hypnotised by the fleeting changes shimmering before her.

His skin now glowed with phosphor, and beneath her caress his flesh seemed to be covered in soft aquamarine scales which made her almost afraid that her touch would hurt him. His eyes, no longer green, shone with the creamy ghost of mother-of-pearl.

He strove deeper within her as they drifted together along the bed of the lake. She felt her orgasm rising up from her womb to her throat and she wanted to open her mouth and cry out — but humans are dumb under water, and she could only express her ecstasy through every cell of her wet skin until the tide of her climax swept through and left her empty. Then Ruari issued a high cetacean sob and withdrew from her suddenly to spend himself in the water. The lake received his fluid and dispersed it through its own body in a milky stream.

She realised she was almost fainting with suffocation.

Rising to the surface she found herself alone again, but she stayed for a while, floating face up to the sky, while the satiated lake flowed tenderly around her pale limbs.

When Julie cleaned the rooms of male guests she thought about Simon as she tidied the intimate cosmetics on the bathroom shelf. Sometimes she even opened a bottle of aftershave and inhaled the deep masculine scent. Once there was a smell that she swore was the same as her father's and again she was drawn back to the memory of rough male cheeks and that last bed-time kiss. But still she did not have the courage to act.

That Christmas Ruth had sent a sweater which was far too big for Julie's thinning body — she'd lost almost twenty pounds since leaving home — and in return Julie sent a card. Just a card. It was all she could bring herself to do.

With the sweater there was also a cheque which represented the last of the maintenance payments. It bought a series of driving lessons and by the following summer she'd passed her test and was ready to go. Except that there wasn't anywhere she wanted to be, other than a very long way away. But she saved hard, and treated herself to her own coming-of-age present — an ancient silver Fiesta, small but flashy. And all hers.

Time to eat. She rolled off the bed and stretched her toes on the threadbare orange carpet. Then she remembered the letter in her overall pocket.

It's strange how sometimes our lives remain static for months or even years and then suddenly events roll into motion so fast we're left breathless by the changes.

And so it was that Simon the money-man had arranged for an endowment policy to mature on Julie's eighteenth birthday. Ruth must have passed on her address, because they wanted to verify her identity before posting the cheque. There was no information about the actual amount, but that mattered to her less than the indirect contact with her father. It had to be sign that something was going to happen.

She sat down immediately and wrote a reply. The wheels were in motion. Within a fortnight she was not only one thousand pounds richer, but she had also written to Simon and received a cautious letter in reply. He turned out to be living a long way north, on the West coast of Scotland. How far that was she had no idea, having only been to Scotland once on that last dreadful holiday with Ruth. She wrote to him again, and he replied again. This time, he invited her to visit.

Well, it's now or never. One Saturday morning in early December she threw a bag into the silver car and set off.

On that same morning Ruth, shipwrecked, turns away from her bedroom window.

She feels like Robinson Crusoe washed up in his own home.

There have been floods before, but never like this. The water swirls dirtily around the hill bringing all manner of offerings to the foot of the house, but she is disinclined to accept them.

Instead, she throws herself on her unmade bed and day-dreams in the half-light of a wet sky. She is trying to summon Ruari back but this time he refuses to come. It had been easy to imagine him before when he was comforting her with food and attention, but now — now she's not quite sure what she needs. And she has to know otherwise she can't cast the spell.

Cast the spell!

It sounds like a fairy tale. But life isn't like that. If she really could weave magic she would have him here with her now. In the flesh. But that has never happened. For two years Ruth has held his memory sealed inside her, and in that form he has not aged. And never will. He will go on and on for ever, being the same.

But Julie has changed. Julie is different now from when she was a lovable tiny child. Ruth sighs. As Ruari has grown more real, her daughter has become a ghost. These days she never phones. Hardly ever writes - and when she does she's cold and unpleasant.

Thank God, then, for Ruari, her own sweet lover...

Abruptly she is startled by an abrupt burst of wind as it clatters against the window.

But it's only the storm.

She reaches out and pulls open a drawer to find the photograph where she captured his image that day on the boat. The picture is fuzzy and indistinct but the lighthouse in the background shows as clear as a ship's bell.

She replaces the worn print into its envelope and rolls over onto her stomach. Maybe the picture will work now and bring him back to her. With her right hand between her legs she closes her eyes tightly and begins to rub as if her clitoris were a genie's lamp. But the space behind her eyelids remains black and she's forced to continue alone until her body shivers in a half-climax and she gives up, unsatisfied and angry.

Oh, why is he so reluctant?

Flinging herself off the crumpled bed she returns to the window. No change. The grey water still streams past the house.

But wait.

In the distance she can see an inflatable dinghy riding amongst the broken wardrobes. And inside it, a man and a smaller figure — perhaps a child, or a woman.

Ruth forces open the window against the gale and shouts at the top of her lungs:

'Help! Over here!'

The dinghy swings about in the swell and seems to be coming towards her.

'Help me!'

Her face contorts in the rain and she can hardly see. Grabbing a yellow blouse from a chair she waves it madly until they look up at her window and his voice cuts through her own.

'Help!'

That's what he's shouting too.

'Help! Hel...' The last part of the word is cut off as the inflatable suddenly begins to spin above a hidden whirlpool.

He wants her to rescue them! That's a joke.

Then she sees that they have no oars. They're sitting inches deep in water and desperately bailing out the flood as fast as it pours into the boat.

Rope.

She runs downstairs to find a length of strong line and races into what's left of her garden. Half of it is underwater now.

They still call to her as she wades in as deep as she dares and coils the rope for throwing — then she stops in amazement and strains to see them more closely.

Who are these people in the dinghy? They look just like...

He is thirty-ish, short-haired, his face flushed with exertion. And the girl — she's just like Julie — but not Julie now. Julie when she was at school. Julie before she left...

'Julie!' she cries. 'Simon! Wait!'

They have come to her together, bringing back the past. How things were, and how they could have been.

'Help us!' they cry. The dinghy is shipping water fast. 'Throw the rope!'

She's been wasting precious moments just standing there, trying to understand, while they're sinking into the filthy water.

She gathers the line and throws as hard as she can, but it's nowhere near long enough. She throws again, and again, hurling it into the jaws of the wind.

But now they have stopped spinning. The whirlpool has pushed them away and they're on the move again, rapidly floating downstream, still calling out. The dinghy is low in the water but it remains upright. She continues to reel in the line and throw it out, although it's becoming increasingly pointless.

There's no more shouting now. They've given her up and are concentrating on bailing with their cupped hands as the inflatable swerves in the current and they disappear behind a group of poplars.

And the river rushes on.

Ruth's hands let go of the rope, letting it sink into the mud, then she picks her way back to the house through a sodden garden which even Noah wouldn't recognize.

Is the incessant rain driving her crazy? It had looked like them — Simon as he was when he left, and the Julie of ten years ago — and she had been unable to save them. Perhaps she is still lying on her bed, having a nightmare.

But the house is solid enough, and once again her clothes are wet enough, to convince her she's awake.

That's what comes of trying to make spells from the past.

This time she doesn't even bother to pull off her sodden clothes, but sinks to her knees before the fire with the dog and dozing hens.

While she sleeps the rain slows until suddenly the sky has emptied itself and a stillness falls instead.

Slowly, tentatively, a blackbird begins to sing as if dawn has only just broken. Its clear tones ripple over the debris.

Although the torrent continues to rush past the garden it seems to have less urgency than before and there is no longer a wind to drive it.

Now comes an empty bed

now a haystack

now an upturned pram

The pram jumps into Ruth's sleep and becomes a rush basket containing Moses, the child of promise.

In her dream she runs to rescue him but she pulls the basket from the water with such haste that it tips and the babe falls among the reeds. As she scrabbles to find him her dream changes and she is searching in the blueness of an indoor swimming pool.

He drifts down and down, his white nappy flowing around his tiny hips, and even though she swims towards him he remains ever out of reach. She can hear the bubbles in her ears and her eyes sting with chlorine but every time she kicks her feet to propel herself in his direction the force of her body in the water pushes him still farther away.

His eyes are dreamy with drowning and his toothless mouth hangs open like a filter-feeder as he sinks lower and lower into the water.

When at last she manages to grab the tail of the napkin it unravels itself to reveal that the child is actually a girl. Shock and surprise force Ruth to the surface for more air, but when she dives again the baby has gone. She swims along the flat bottom painted blue with yellow lines, but the child is nowhere to be seen.

Sobbing in her sleep she dives swims searches, dives swims searches as the flood glides past and takes away

the pram

a calf with no head

a velvet armchair

a guitar

and a swirling mass of blue underwear.

Meanwhile, the air outside is suddenly dense with the noise of engines. A helicopter is following the torrent towards the brick house standing above the flood. The pilot circles downwards to look for movement and finds a thin column of smoke rising from the chimney.

He takes his loud-hailer.

IS ANYBODY THERE?

But the sound of his voice is lost in the bubbles of Ruth's underwater ears and she does not hear him.

He decides the smoke must be coming from a deserted fireplace, regains altitude, and sweeps on, only to slow again when he passes the pram. But there is no sign of life there either.

With the departure of the helicopter the blackbird renews her song and coaxes the grey sky into revealing a pallid sun.

When Ruth awakes from her sleep by the fireplace she sees that the door is open and a mild yellow glow falls into the room.

There is no sound of the rain, but she can hear the clucking of the hens as they wander in and out, their claws leaving muddy stars on the carpet, and the sound of humming from the kitchen tells her that Ruari is back.

He brings clothes to replace the wet ones she has slept in and,

103

after helping her to her feet, gently lifts her jumper above her head and slides away her trousers. Like a child she stands for a moment in her knickers before the fire while he unfolds the dry clothes and helps her put them on.

This time, however, she is unreceptive to his attentions. She allows him to dress her but remains sullen and unresponsive. He had refused to be there when she needed him and now her longing is transmuted into anger, and she averts her eyes resentfully as he fits warm socks onto her feet. One foot... other foot...

When he has completed his task she sweeps poultry dung from the nearest chair and sits down heavily, still avoiding his eye. But he moves over to the window to gaze silently at the coursing water below. The lake — his fragment of ocean — where they had so many times joined together is now no more than a swelling in the main body of the river.

He stands for a long time, transfixed and unable to tear his eyes from the buried lake which pulls him with such power, while she in turn scrutinizes the slump of his shoulders. This is the first time she has ever observed a change in him, and it is as if his energy is slowly seeping away.

Against the light he looks transparent, almost ghostly. as if he is disappearing by the minute...

...then he turns to face her, his pallid features curved into a sad smile. She waits, certain she knows what he is about to say, convinced that he intends to join the fast-receding torrent and return to his proper element. For this reason she is taken by surprise when he finally speaks.

'When was the last time you heard from Julie?'

'What?'

In truth it has been a long time. She will not calculate exactly how long, but she is surprised at the rush of emotion brought on by his question. She cannot help it. Her face crumples suddenly into angry tears.

'I don't want to talk about that.'

Ruari has become enough. She has made him, forced him, to be enough, and he has duly expanded to fill all the empty spaces in her heart.

He leaves the window and moves towards her in gentle supplication — 'Why don't you get in touch?'

'There's no point. You don't understand. Why don't you leave me alone?'

Scrambling to her feet she rushes outside to escape him. Why try

104

to change when so many things are already fixed? And Julie...
Julie has her own life now.

She joins the hens who are scavenging for drowned worms, and
finds that the flood-tide has carried back all the stones she'd picked
up from the garden the week before.

Crouching down amongst the birds, she begins again. But as
she scrambles in the mud she suddenly remembers, unbidden,
that when her daughter cried like this she used to soothe her
with ancient stories.

That seems like a long time ago.

But now, one of those stories comes back to her almost word
for word, and she can hear her own voice singing in her head as
she used to tell it when she held Julie in her arms and rocked
away the tears.

It is the story of the selkie wife...

*Finning in the deep dark hollows of the ocean I remember the
sadness of human mothers and I cry for my children, because
once, I, too was a woman.*

*It was Midsummer when the moon beckoned through the waves
and called us to dance. I was young then, my teats hardly ripened
for pups, and the joy of the night filled me when we rose up to the
surface and into the moonglow. In the distance the white sands
lay empty as we hurried towards them, and on reaching the rocky
shores we pulled off our furry pelts so they would not weigh us
down while we danced. The air blew coolly on our under-skins,
but we soon became warm as we swung together around the moonlit
pools, laughing and shouting to the beat of the waves. Our skins
lay on the rocks, their wetness shining in the dark, and their scent
filled the air with the aroma of harbours.*

*Suddenly one of us cried out. There was a human man crouching
in the shadows. Spying on us!*

*We ran helter-skelter towards our furs. Without them we
wouldn't be able to get back.*

Faster!

*Slipping them on, cold and heavy, and diving from the rocks
into the rolling waves and away.*

I ran too.

But my skin was gone!

It must have been washed away by the cruel waves. By now I was the last one. Beyond the rocks, dark heads bobbed in the water, and I could hear them calling to me.

Hurry!

Quickly!

I would have to leave it behind. I didn't think. I just fled and dived below the waters.

But the sea refused me.

It entered my throat and choked me. It tangled in my unwieldy legs and pulled me under until I could not breathe. As I struggled I could see my family watching in horror. I began to drown, and they could not rescue me.

Then the ocean gave me a last chance.

Picking me up in its frothy arms it hurled me back onto the sand and there, waiting, was the human-man.

He spoke, but I could not understand him. I wailed for my people as he gathered me up.

'Wait!' I cried. 'Let me try again!'

But he did not know my language either, only answering my plea with soothing murmurs until I fell unconscious in his dry cold arms.

When I awoke, I was burning. In front of me a monster roared with such heat as is never found in the cold Atlantic. My under-skin was red and sore and I pulled myself away until I reached a cool corner in the shadows.

The human-man brought me fish and water. I ate the fish fast, but I could not drink the water. It had no salt. Instead, I threw it on my skin to heal the burning.

And so I lay, all day, until the evening rain began. The air around me was heavy and strong but beyond an opening there was water falling from the sky and I crawled towards it until I was rolling in mud, and sobbing my loss to the waning moon.

He stood at the opening watching and his face looked much as if it held love. Then he took off his skins — which were many — and crawled down with me in the mud to share my sadness.

That night I learned how to love him.

The years passed. Twice I went to the water's edge to give birth to a child with slick black hair. They both swam like fish almost before they could walk. Dark beauties, my boy and girl.

Only when Midsummer's Eve came round each year did my pain break out, and then my restless sleep was broken by the mutterings of cockles and the whistling of dolphins. I would dream of my family and wonder if they had survived the trawls for yet

106

another year.

Then the next evening I would slip away from my sleeping babes and go to the shore to greet the others. They no longer ventured on to the sand to dance but they would gather beyond the rocks and call to me across the waves. They were still searching for my skin.

Over the years my human-man taught me his language and in return I gave him some of our words. When he took out his boat at night he called to the seals and they answered because they knew he belonged to me.

But none of us were aware he had a secret.

While he kept it, our children grew. The girl was always bright and quick, the boy a spark of pleasure — oh, it cuts my heart to remember them.

Then one day they were playing beneath an old hulk half-buried in the sands, while I gathered sea-grass for baskets. That year they had turned seven and nine.

My youngest came running to me.

'There's an animal over here! Come and see!'

She tugged my arm and I followed. Sometimes I wish I hadn't because there, hidden under the hulk beneath a white stone was my skin. It was wrapped in a piece of fishing-net.

Then I knew.

I lifted the stone and held the skin to my cheek. It still smelled of sea-birds and harbours, and my salt-tears dampened it as I keened for my home. Then there was a shout, and my human-husband was running towards us.

'No!' he was shouting. 'Don't!'

But I pulled off the net and ran to the sea, stumbling through the dunes, the land-bound marram grass slashing at my legs to keep me back.

And the children were running behind me, wailing with terror. I hesitated.

Then I ran faster. I had no choice. I ran away from them.

He sped over the sand calling 'Forgive me!'

But I could not.

As I reached the rocks I could hardly breathe while I threw off my blue dress and struggled into the skin. It hung heavy on my limbs, but in a moment I was ready to dive.

I hurled myself into the water, sped down to the deeps and then rose again to look at the shore.

My beautiful children sobbed in his arms and he still cried out,

107

over and over again 'I'm sorry! I loved you! I'm sorry!'

But as the brine filled my ears I found I could no longer understand their speech. It joined with the howl of the wind and the tears of the salt-spray, and I dived deep again.

Now I no longer dance on the shores.

I will never,

ever,

cast off my skin again.

Sometimes his boat comes to these lonely rocks and I hear all three of them calling and crying for me above the waves.

But selkies live out their whole lives in a pool of tears.

As Ruth crawls her way across the mud, her head singing with long-forgotten stories of despair, Julie drives north through the vacuum locks of England's corridors.

The rainstorm continues moving eastward, away from her route and heading deeper into the land-locked Midlands where Ruth struggles alone with her solitary fantasies.

At this point, Simon has many more years to live.

But which Simon are we talking about here? For there are surely two of him. There is the 'real' one, the man who many years before said goodbye to his only daughter and set off to start a new life with a new wife, and there is Julie's Dad, who has more in common with Ruari than she would ever admit, but with rather more unpleasant results.

Julie's Dad is a composite of all the men she's ever met. He is the boy in the car, and the boy by the lake. He is the kindly hotel porter who'd taken her under his wing when she first left home, and he is the stern maitre d' who docks your wages if you break so much as a single wine-glass.

All of her life she's been fitting him together like a jigsaw, and by now the puzzle is pretty well complete, although deep in her heart she knows it can't help her. When the time comes, she'll have to tip all the pieces back in the box and start again.

Meanwhile, as she drives carefully down the slow lane of the motorway, she forces herself to recognize that she isn't only a novice driver — she is a novice daughter as well. Many dangers lie in wait for her, and well she knows it.

The features which make up Simon come from everywhere. They're not simple physical characteristics — she has old photos for that. Of course, he'll surely have aged a bit but he can't have changed too drastically from the dapper, tidy man of the albums. Pale, slightly freckled skin and thin sandy hair. A slight body, unused to heavy physical labour, with narrow shoulders and skinny hips. Weak, almost ineffective in appearance...

But no, that's not right. He was strong. He used to lift her as though she weighed nothing, and the grip of his hand on her shoulder when she'd been naughty was painfully firm. Of course, she was only very small, but his rare bouts of anger had been utterly terrifying. She used to cower — yes, she remembers this now — she used to cower on Ruth's knee while he berated them both for all sorts of inconsequential little crimes.

His face suddenly slots onto that of someone she saw in the hotel only last week. The man had been taking a pre-dinner drink with his wife and two small sons when one of the boys rose to his feet rather clumsily and tipped the small table, glasses and all, onto the carpeted floor. Ruth, passing by with an armful of towels, had time to capture only a snapshot image of the scene: the child transfixed with fear, the brother the same, and the woman in the act of leaping anxiously to help, her eyes averted from her red-faced husband whose hand was raised, flat open as if to strike, while his son made no move to escape.

Ruth caught that little family tableau and stored it in her jigsaw. She already had a good collection:

The man who ripped up his girlfriend's clothes and threw them out of the hotel window because she'd smiled at the wine waiter.

The man (it had been in all the papers) who crept into his three year-old daughter's bedroom, forced a bottle into her vagina then masturbated over her face.

The man who loved his woman so deeply he had to strangle her (thank God, thought Julie, that no man loves me that much).

The man in every cellar all over the world who tortures children with pliers and electrodes and scalpels to make them tell him a truth. Any truth.

The man who thieves and cuts and shoots and rapes and

mutilates until he forms 95% of the prison population but who is not a natural criminal. Society only made him like that.

The man husband, father, son, brother, lover who twists the minds of girls and women until they're ready to believe for him that night is day.

The man who entices another into a public toilet then grinds his face into the floor for the entertainment of his macho friends.

The man (the author) who sells his grubby stories of money and fighting and hungry cunts gasping for sex and calls it Realism.

The man whose pit-bull terrier in its spiked collar is even uglier than he is.

The man who sits at a table and starts wars.

The man who fights them for him in the name of all the mothers and children who would really rather he didn't bother, actually.

The man in a suit who sells baby milk way past its sell-by date to a black woman with empty breasts, and then adds the cost to the Third World Debt.

The man warm, lovable, fatherly and generous, who one day just ups and changes his mind and leaves
and leaves
and leaves
and leaves...

You can't cry and drive at the same time.

Julie pulls into a service area and turns off the engine. On the damp tarmac two small boys are stamping on slugs and sliding over the sticky corpses.

She locks the car, wipes her eyes, and walks to the toilets through a car-park full of HGVs, the cab of each one festooned with pictures of tits.

She's driven too far without a break. She is over-tired and

110

allowing herself to become ridiculously emotional. After all, not every man could be so bad. But then, how would she know? She's never known a single individual male human being with any sort of intimacy, so all she can do is judge them by their actions, and to be honest the picture doesn't look good.

But she wants things to go well with Simon, she really does. Ruth has become impenetrable and locked away in her own head — thus, in a way, her mother has deserted her as well... but no, in all honesty she can't quite substantiate that bitter claim. As a child she'd always believed Ruth to be the innocent victim of Simon's capricious selfishness and she still maintains that if he hadn't gone away Ruth would never have retreated into madness, if that's what it was.

She grins ruefully as she walks back to the car. Perhaps her mother is more sane than she gives her credit for. At least she has survived, and that seems quite an achievement on its own. And, thinks Julie, she may be crazy but at least she's happy...

Notes towards Survival

What should you do if you find yourself thrown into the water?

1. *Get out! Water conducts heat much faster than air, and you'll reduce the chance of hypothermia by simply keeping as much of your body as possible out of the water. This will probably mean climbing on to the upturned boat. Bodysize is another factor here. Small people cool faster than large people. Thin people cool faster than fat people. Children cool faster than adults. Because women tend on the whole to be fleshier than men, they also have a higher survival rate.*

2. *Non-swimmers. Try to remain as still as possible. The more you struggle and flail in the water, the faster you'll become exhausted and begin to sink. In addition, movement will cool you down much faster, bringing you closer to hypothermia. Instead it's better to conserve your energy and let your natural buoyancy bring you up to the surface. Then you can try to mimic a corked bottle in one of three ways:*

   a) *Keep your body vertical and your head back, face upwards and out of the water. By pressing your palms downwards you can push your mouth far enough above the water to be able to take short vigorous breaths.*

b) *Tilt your body diagonally, face downwards and the back of your head out of the water. To breathe, kick your legs and press down your hands. Alternately breathe in — out — and duck under the water, then repeat.*

c) *Bring your knees up to your chest and clasp them with both hands. Your spine will show above the water, your head will be submerged near your knees. To breathe, lift your head out of the water and quickly breathe out-and-in. This position is also good for conserving body heat. If you find yourself in the water with other people you can reduce heat loss by huddling together.*

3. *Swimmers. Stay with the boat if possible. This will make it easier for rescuers to find you. Do not swim unless there is absolutely no hope of rescue and you feel certain you can make it without failing from exhaustion or hypothermia. In any case, use a flotation aid. Move slowly and don't fight the current. It's better to swim across it if it looks as though that will bring you nearer the shore.*

4. *Always wear a flotation aid. But it's possible to stay afloat for hours even without a life-jacket, and salt water makes you more buoyant still. You may also be able to make floats out of your clothing, and if you're lucky you may find some debris to cling to. People have been known to drift in the open sea for days before being rescued or carried to shore by the current.*

Handfuls of brown mud.

Rounded stones slipping between her fingers, Ruth makes a pile beside her. Occasionally she finds an interesting pebble and stops to rub it against her trousers until it glows. That one she drops into her pocket.

She keeps her eyes firmly on the ground in case Ruari should be watching

She's decided she doesn't want him.

She doesn't want him any more.

As she works in the mud she mutters to herself, crawling along the ground and hurling stones behind her as she goes. The hens fly up in fright as rocks whiz past their tail-feathers.

Suddenly her progress is halted by a fierce ache beginning at the heart and spreading outwards. Somewhere beneath her ribs there is a lump of pain which swells and hardens by the second.

Any moment now it will burst.

She feels it welling up inside her, growing bigger and bigger until she is forced to rise to her feet and stretch her body to encompass it.

There she stands.

By now the pain has reached the top of her body, but she will not let it out.

It remains contained as her eyes bulge and her cheeks blow out around her lips, pursed tight with the bitterness of so many disappointments. She plants herself firmly in the mud, feet apart for stability and stolid with determination.

She will not give in.

Whatever would happen now if she let out a cry?

It would never stop. It would screech round the house and trees like a screamer balloon and never come back. There would be nothing left.

See her now.

She is bloated with her own isolation.

She is full of the stinking gas of loneliness.

The sort that makes people hold their noses and back off.

See her.

Is she going to break down?

What can she do?

Her lungs shriek at her that she must breathe soon.

She's terrified, but she lets out a gasp of carbon dioxide and inhales a quick rush of air. She manages to do it without allowing anything else either in or out of her body, and he's still there inside her, spreading and inflating within that brittle bone cage.

He's been there for too long. Now something has got to give.

But the trouble is that she believes — she really does believe — that if she lets go she'll never see him again.

Quick! She must make a decision.

The grey water swills around the smashed hen-house at the bottom of the garden as she tries to imagine life without this phantom of her own making, but all she can do is make pictures of his sea-washed face. He's smiling. Blowing her a kiss.

She can't do it.

It's impossible.

She starts to swallow in gulps, pumping the sorrow back where it came from.

She can't live without him, poor substitute though he is.

This decision made, relief begins to seep into her muscles as she squeezes back all the loneliness, all the desire, all the tears, and her heart hardens again under the pressure of its pitiful contents.

There is a need, and she cannot deny it.

For without Ruari, what would her life be?

He steps quietly into the garden and enfolds her in his arms. She no longer weeps but her weight falls against him as if she were dead. And the ghost comforts the corpse as the bloated river carries by a lifeless and unrecognizable animal gruesomely impaled on a shattered wooden spar.

Soon they go upstairs and make love, and afterwards the moonlight falls across the water outside as Ruth drifts into a proper night-time sleep. Today she has travelled the span of her emotions only to return to their starting-point. Exhausted by her circular journey she sinks into the pillows while night takes care of the house, curling itself around the gaping window, and a yellow shirt still hangs across the sill as she rocks into a dream.

Turning the key in the front door she is immediately shaken by the hollow quiet filling the house. A heavy absence clings to the furniture, and a chill pervades the air. A clock ticks, a tap drips.

She pushes her way through the kitchen, through the conservatory and into the garden. Here there are birds — some cheeping and chirping in the spring air; some in pieces on the lawn, their feathers and bones scattered over the grass.

The conservatory, too, houses dead things. There is a pungent odour of rotting vegetation. Begonias, hung basketed above head level, have shrivelled up and died from thirst, and decompose in slimy threads. Webs span every available space in the room, the sucked-out corpses of flies hanging upon the weave. Spiders at the end of their carnivorous course recline on their backs along the windowsills, eight legs folded in to make each body resemble the clenched fist of rigor mortis. Or a sated sun- bather.

Starting at the headlong flight of a daddy-long-legs tangling in her hair, Ruth the dreamer turns back through the peeling red door and into the kitchen where she smells coffee. She goes through the hall and then upstairs to her dead mother's bedroom.

Now she stands before the mirror. Her clothes lie on the floor, and instead she wears her mother's navy trousers, pulled down at the instep by black elastic straps, and a yellow polka-dot blouse tucked into a broad belt. Her hair is waved and lacquered, her eyes painted pastel blue.

Ruth the dreamer looks at her reflection and wonders who she really is.

She turns sideways before the mirror and throws back her head coquettishly, puffs delicately at a cigarette, and smiles like her mother used to.

What was it she used to say?

Smoke jets from her nostrils — a sophisticated female dragon — as she mouths out the words:

'We all need someone to love, Ruth.'

Someone to love.

Someone to love.

Now she is outside and she's pushing forward into a force ten gale. It pounds, terrifyingly loud, inside her skull, but through the wind she can just make out the sound of another voice and she knows she should be listening but the storm blocks it out...

The river is subsiding, but inside Ruth's sleep the torrent rages on.

Someone should be here to lift away a wisp of hair from her face and gently pull up the quilt around her shoulders, but there is no-one else.

And meanwhile, her history streams by...

When she was a child, Ruth was silent for much of the time.

This is how it went.

Ruth's mum was called Rosie, and her dad was called Jack.

Jack grew up in a small colliery village where mining had brought up the skin of the landscape in shining black welts. He entered the pit as soon as he left school, so when the Second World War broke out he found himself in a reserved occupation and ineligible for the front. Since he was of a retiring nature, and had no desire to die in a foreign land, this arrangement suited him very well.

After the war, in 1947, he was working underground when a coal-cart fell on his leg, and upon returning to work after a lengthy convalescence he found he had been transferred to the pit-head office. It was comfortable for him there. Indoor work, sheltered from the mud and damp, and he could bury his head in his ledgers and keep himself to himself. After a few years he moved to a better job with the county council where he stayed, happily content, for the remainder of his working life.

Through those years the main source of his contentment was Rosie.

One evening in the autumn of 1944, when he was still employed underground, Jack took his dog for a walk across the stubbly corn-fields beyond the slag-heaps. By the third field the colliery had fallen out of sight and he was just beginning to feel relaxed when he saw a group of ruddy-cheeked land-girls tying sheaves and loading them onto a trailer. Naturally shy, he prepared to make a detour around the women. He'd heard stories of their teasing banter and he knew his timid repartee would not stand up to this sort of encounter.

However there was to be no escape because as he edged along the hedgerow a tousled head suddenly popped up on the other side and gave a little scream.

'You didn't tell me there was someone coming, you buggers!' she bawled furiously at the other girls, who stood clutching their sides with laughter some distance away in the centre of the field.

Rosie fastened up her dungarees and shook her fist at her friends, while Jack blushed scarlet and looked the other way.

'Um — sorry,' he mumbled. 'Didn't see you there.'

'I should hope you didn't!' she retorted. 'You weren't peeping were you?'

As she spoke she crawled through a jagged hole in the hedge and then scrambled to her feet in front of him. Stalks of wheat hung in her dark curly hair.

'Course I wasn't.' He thought he would die of embarrassment.

'Well, that's alright then!' she grinned. 'Got to go. Ta-ra!'

He watched her run back to the others, one dungaree strap flapping loose behind her, her boots crunching in the stubble. As her laughter flew back to him in the breeze he fell in love simply and immediately.

They were married a few weeks after Armistice day. At the church the land-girls formed an arch of honour with their pitch-forks, and Rosie giggled her way through the celebrations until bed-time, when they turned to more serious pleasures. The next morning Jack awoke to see her sleeping face on the pillow beside him and he knew he was the happiest man alive.

They made a traditional couple. After the wedding Rosie took to cooking and cleaning as if she had never driven a tractor in her life, and Jack went off to the pit every day, his snap-tin bulging with slabs of home-cooked meat-and-potato pie. When she'd kissed him goodbye Rosie donned her flowery pinafore to clean the grate, sweep the floors, do the washing, and stretch her back to ease the weight of Ruth, who was pushing up inside her like a ripening ear of corn.

In 1946 Ruth was born.

In 1947 the coal-cart fell onto Jack's leg and he was confined to bed for three months. Ruth passed much of that time alone in her pram downstairs whilst her parents found a few more interesting ways to make love, and by the time Jack started his new job at the colliery office Rosie was pregnant again.

These were the days when children were seen and not heard, so it was with a clear conscience that Rosie left Ruth marooned in her pram for hours on end while she and the invalid Jack frolicked in his sick-bed.

The simple truth was that they just couldn't keep their hands off each other.

Rosie loved his broad endless shoulders laced black with unwashable rivulets of coal-dust. She liked to nuzzle down into his rough chest and slide her tongue around his nipple until his breath caught in his throat. He might be shy in public, but in private his sensuality overcame his diffidence and for the rest of his life he found infinite variations in the thrill of their love-making.

His bad leg made it impossible for him to descend the stairs, so she emptied his pot and brought him his meals on a tray. But so many times, the meal would be left to go cold as the sight of her made him rise under the bed-clothes. Then she would hitch up her skirt and sit astride him as he lay immobilised, holding the

117

curve of her sex just above his reach and pushing minted new potatoes between his lips while he stretched towards her.

'Just one more mouthful!' she would laugh. 'You've got to build up your strength!'

'Mmm — no — no more — ah!' Suddenly she sunk herself onto him and he almost choked on the last buttery mouthful.

He gasped as she moved on top of him, squeezing him inside her and raising her eyes to the ceiling.

Then — 'Is that her crying?'

They stopped and listened. Every second of immobility fired the desire between them, whilst a distant wail rose from the kitchen.

'She'll be alright for another minute.'

And so they would pump and writhe and drip with craving for each other, their ears blocked by passion, trying to wait until they could climax together in the final thrust and squeeze of love.

And in the kitchen, Ruth, sensing she was being left out of something, wailed herself into silence. Eventually Rosie would come back down the narrow stairs and call up to Jack

'Well, she's stopped now anyway.'

In her pram Ruth wore a set of reins which bounded her chest and shoulders. Clips underneath the arms were attached to the inner bars so that she could sit up or lie on her back, but rolling over or climbing out were impossible. Early on, however, she discovered there was another way to reach the ground.

One day, after a bout of powerful struggling and screaming she found that by rocking sideways back and forth she could overbalance the pram. It tipped up, falling onto the linoleum with a crash, its screaming captive trapped inside with her face pressed against the cold metallic supports of the hood.

This time the noise was too much to ignore, and Rosie ran downstairs without her knickers to right the pram and comfort its distraught occupant.

Ruth didn't try that trick again, and as the weeks passed she learned slowly and painfully that there was no point in crying for attention. Her mother would only come when she was good and ready, and not before. That's how it was for children then. It was policy to ignore them, but this was done only in their best interests. It would do no good for a child to acquire an inflated sense of her own importance.

Seen and not heard.

So it was not surprising that Ruth was not heard when in 1948 Jennifer arrived on the scene, the product of all those hot dinners gone cold on the tray. By now Ruth was nearly two, and a model child. She smiled and said please-and-thank-you whenever propriety demanded, and she had learned only to cry for visible injuries which could be easily salved with pink Germolene. She had deeper pains too, but they did not respond to ointment so it seemed pointless to express them.

1950.

Ruth is four, Jennifer two. And Jack finds that his time at the pithead office has stood him in good stead for a clerical position with the council. They can even afford a mortgage. Just before Ruth is due to start school they move house to a town with no slag-heaps and lots of trees. New suburbs are mushrooming everywhere, and Jack and Rosie buy a nice semi with a bit of garden.

Jack spends a weekend putting up a fence around the plot so that Ruth and Jennifer will be totally safe. He builds a sand-pit and seeds a lawn.

Then the girls are sent out to play.

Many years later as Ruth watched Julie with her doll's teacups on the lawn, she recalled that she and Jennifer seemed to have spent their entire childhood being sent out to play. Sometimes they would try to get into the house to use the toilet only to find the back-door locked, especially on Sunday afternoons when Jack retired for a nap and Rosie always, mysteriously, decided to tidy upstairs at the same time. Over the years their daughters acquired a favourite corner of the garden for weeing, but as they crouched down trying not to get their socks wet, they never guessed that it was in that position their mother first saw their father strolling along on the other side of a hawthorn hedge.

In truth, Rosie considered herself blessed with all she'd ever wanted. Jack had provided a pleasant house and a regular income, but more than that he had become the sum focus of her sexual and emotional life. In bed he was passionate and needy, out of bed he was calm and undemanding. And why should he not be? Life required little of him other than that he should remain at his desk between the hours of nine and five-thirty for five days a week, fifty weeks of the year (excluding public holidays). Beyond that, his time was his own. He was not required to wash, cook, or look after his children other than the occasional game of snap. Of course, had he fathered sons it would have been a different story, and he would have become involved in fishing trips and football and adventures in meccano. As it was, he was unfitted to participate in anything his daughters might need to know about so he was let off the hook.

He grew a few vegetables at the back, kept the front plot neat, and redecorated the house now and then. He'd never learned to drive, so there was no car to tinker with on Saturday mornings, although he did sometimes take his bike to pieces and put it back together again. Rosie's tractor skills had long been forgotten, and the idea that she might be able to drive a family car seems never to have been discussed.

Rosie did not go out to work. After passing through the arch of the land-girls' pitchforks she didn't earn another pay cheque for the rest of her life. Once Jack had changed jobs for the last time, she knew she would never have to clock on or stand behind a shop counter. And activities with pitch-forks were, naturally, right out of the question.

So there they were.

It was the nineteen fifties, and each year brought something new into Rosie's pretty kitchen. A gas cooker. A twin tub. An electric toaster which sometimes got stuck and filled the room with acrid smoke. Rosie ironed school dresses, and washed, and cooked, and cleaned, and always put on fresh lipstick just before Jack pedalled home from the office.

Rosie and Jack were a popular couple in their street. The other wives found Jack handsome and sometimes they fantasised about his miner's body while they lay beside their husbands who in turn were busy fantasising about Rosie singing like Polly Garter at her washing line (although unfortunately for them she did not share Polly's line in morals). The women found in Rosie a trusted confidante, but when they whispered veiled hints about their unsatisfactory private lives Rosie only ever smiled sympathetically without offering a comparable complaint in return. Sometimes they wondered maliciously whether she was hiding secret agonies behind her discretion, but mostly they just reluctantly assumed she had no problems in the bedroom area.

In that, they were correct.

And the men, helped by Jack to fix a slipping roof-tile or build a paddling pool for the kids, thought the same. Anyone would be happy, they thought, with a wife like Rosie wearing the lacy knickers they saw on the line when they popped over to borrow a No.5 drill bit.

It was true.

Rosie and Jack were content. They'd got more than they'd ever expected to have, and two lovely daughters as well.

Ruth and Jennifer grew up in this calm and settled home. How perfect. The family lived sensibly within their means, taking an annual sea-side holiday and spending Christmas with each set of grandparents on alternating years. We won't go into details about the grandparents — you've got to stop somewhere, and Rosie and Jack had jettisoned their roots anyway when they left the colliery village. Christmas visits were only made out of duty, and the girls followed their parents' example by being polite but unforthcoming to their relatives.

Not that there were any indiscretions to be made, but even the smallest amount of knowledge is power.

Knowledge is power. And as their mother, Rosie was of course in an ideal position to know everything about her daughters and to use this prerogative as she saw fit. However, she chose to decline the opportunity.

As long as the girls were well-presented and obedient, her interest in them went little further. This might perhaps have been acceptable if Ruth and Jennifer had been able to create their own small citadel within the house, but unfortunately that was not possible.

The two girls were very different indeed.

Ruth, as we have seen, dealt in silence. Adopted initially as a protective position, it later became a tactic for hostility too. She was very good at refusing to communicate, and she used this facility in varying degrees.

With Jennifer it was easy. Ruth simply refused to say a word for days on end, a reproof particularly potent since they shared a bedroom and her silent hostility intensified with physical proximity. Jennifer could howl, cry, beg or bribe, but Ruth would remain silent until her desire for vengeance was thoroughly satisfied.

Dealings with Rosie and Jack, however, required a more subtle approach. Ruth could not simply refuse to speak to her parents since the punishment for such rudeness was prompt and painful — a smack on the back of the legs seems to have been the most commonly used method. No, with her parents Ruth learned to maintain a veneer of civility as if nothing was wrong, whilst at the same time withholding small items of information which would have passed unnoticed anyway. In this way it affected no-one but herself, but for her it served as a satisfyingly private revenge.

She would simply not tell them if she'd come top in a class test, or been picked for the school quiz team, and what they didn't know they didn't miss. Her recriminations took the form of deliberate omissions, and we can see now with hindsight that this was probably the most appropriate revenge, since they themselves had hurt her most by their own disinterest.

Especially Rosie. Jack hardly counted, being a generally invisible person anyway.

Rosie was tactless. She rarely showed any interest in little Ruth's clumsy attempts at art work. When pushed for an opinion she might say something like: 'Is that an apple? I thought it was a football', and that would be the limit of it.

She was also guilty of the heinous sin of family treason. Chatting over the garden fence, she would make the neighbours laugh with stories about the foolish side of Ruth's nature, but never remembered to mention her achievements.

At home, she often pretended she was listening when she wasn't. How many heartfelt confidences did Ruth pour into her mother's ear before she realised that Rosie was paying no attention at all and within a few minutes would have forgotten the conversation?

But worst of all, it was patently clear to both children that Rosie loved Jack best. She always had, and she always would.

This was the biggest sin, but Rosie would defend it to her dying day.

'Of course I loved your father — I chose to marry him didn't I? He was there before you ever came on the scene, so what do you expect? Anyway, it's not my responsibility. We did the job of bringing you up, now it's up to you to find your own love in life.'

Often Ruth would walk into a room to find her parents embracing. Sometimes her father had her hand up her mother's skirt. Rosie would turn to her daughter and say with a sickly smile

'We all need someone to love, Ruth. Aren't I lucky I've got your Dad?'

Ruth hated it. She wanted to shout

'But what about me?'

Of course, she never did.

Jennifer's experience of her parents was little different from Ruth's, but this younger child was of a much more pragmatic nature. She spent most of her time playing outside with a gaggle of friends, so that by the time she reached her teens she was hardly ever at home. And, if her parents only knew it, hardly ever at school either. As soon as she could she joined the Army and was subsequently rarely seen in the town again.

122

Jennifer found Ruth's silent fury towards their parents very tiresome.

'If you don't like it — leave!' she would say. 'I do. Just go out and let them get on with it. They're so wrapped up in themselves they never notice if we're here or not anyway. You're just gutless,' she would add when Ruth shook her head. 'You're too scared to stand on your own two feet.'

Sometimes Jennifer embarked on huge rows with their parents which lasted for days and days. Ruth would stay in their bedroom pretending to read while the furore raged on downstairs.

But Jennifer's arguments were never about the paucity of her family life — this she accepted this as normal. Her frustrations related to more materialistic topics — the money for a new dress or permission to go to an all-night party, and in many ways they were pointless, circular quarrels since Jennifer always ended up doing what she wanted to anyway.

Ruth never involved herself like that. She disliked disagreements, if only because she was afraid that once she opened her mouth in anger she might never be able to stop. The strength of her own emotions scared her, but what frightened her even more was that she didn't really know what she was so upset about. The memories ran so deep that they had become no more than jagged layers of minerals in the strata of her personality. She had no conscious recollection of the upturned pram, for instance, and even now she remains unaware of it.

So the possibility of an affinity with Jennifer, which might have been a refuge for Ruth, never materialised. Instead, studying took its place.

While Jennifer spent her adolescence hurtling from one social scene to the next, Ruth stayed at home and read books until one day she found herself in university digs and finally realised there might be other ways of life in the world.

The only light in the darkness of her teens had been the boy to whom she gave her virginity. Then after him, a long period with no-one.

The boy was important because he understood. Another seen-but-not-heard baby, he recognized her silence as the same as his own and they formed a clumsy inarticulate relationship where gestures of affection were strangely absent. They felt very comfortable together.

Then his parents moved away, and since he was only fifteen he had to go with them. Ruth was alone again. However he left her with a grain of consolation — the knowledge that she was not completely crazy and that there were other people in the world like her.

She clung to that raft for a very long time.

The Cowfish is well-protected from predators. Its whole body, except for the fins and mouth, is encased in a box of bone.

Jack died.

Sitting at his desk at work he had reached for his coffee cup and suddenly keeled over with a heart attack. There seemed to be no reason for his sudden illness, but it happened too fast for Rosie to cope with. A few months later Ruth graduated from university but her mother felt unable to attend the ceremony without her beloved husband.

Ruth understood.

Well, of course she did. She was the best-placed person in the world to appreciate what Jack had meant to Rosie. Full of sympathy, and hoping secretly to get close to her mother at last, she moved back home for a while to look after her.

She wasn't needed.

Rosie shut herself in her bedroom all day and looked at photos. She was not yet fifty, and she had nothing left to live for. Ruth pottered about downstairs, making meals her mother would not eat, afraid to put on the TV in case she was accused of being insensitive to a widow's pain.

Eventually she gave up and went back to her own flat, disappointed.

Rosie lived on for another five years then suddenly developed a very fast cancer which killed her within a matter of months, and she was glad to go. She'd been waiting a long time to be relieved of her loneliness.

At the time when their mother was admitted to hospital Jennifer was stationed in Germany and could not come, so Simon reluctantly took a few days' leave from the bank to look after Julie while Ruth sat at her mother's bedside. He found the time useful for secretly putting his affairs in order prior to making his getaway.

Ruth held her mother's hand for many long hours, but Rosie didn't recognize her and kept calling for Jack. Ruth had to bite her tongue to keep herself from insisting

'But I'm here Mum...'

as she had always had to do.

I'm here Mum.

Look at me, Mum.

Look at me.

Yes, look at her.

There she weeps as she sleeps as she rocks on her downy pillow towards the morning while outside the flood seeps away slowly, innocuously, beyond the four walls.

It was not until long after Rosie died, after Simon left, after Alex, that Ruth took control of her life. As the years passed the hedge of thorny roses grew higher around the house where mother and daughter lived together in perfect contentment.

Their home was set in an ocean of shops and streets. A modernised end-terrace where the heavy feet of the neighbours could be heard on the stairs next door and dogs barked alone in the echoing traffic-free dead of night.

In this forest of bricks and replacement windows, Ruth's house made the tail-end of the row into a flame of summer colour with its garlands of pink ramblers climbing around a precarious complexity of trellis work.

This little family of two had many of the securities we all so desire. A regular income with long holidays. Decent food and clothes. A VW Polo with a sunroof. A small but productive vegetable garden. Central heating with constant hot water, and wall-to-wall carpet in every room.

The house was small, just two down and two up, but since mother and daughter enjoyed each other's company there were seldom quarrels over space. And there was no spare bedroom tempting visitors to outstay their welcome.

After she had planted the roses, Ruth drew herself in, squeezing into a confined but cosy space, and firmly shut the front door.

Of course, she was accustomed to this intimacy. The bedroom she had shared with Jennifer for so many years may not always have been a happy place, but at least it was secure. Its boundaries were close at hand and utterly tangible.

But every now and then Ruth and Julie were visited by a demon who hinted that maybe their life was not so perfect after all.

When she was eight, Julie joined the Brownies. At first Ruth thought this was a good idea, since Julie would make friends and get out and about. But very soon afterwards came the weekend camps then, horror of horrors, long summer camps. One week. Two weeks. Within a year Julie never seemed to be at home. Church parades, bazaars, weekly meetings. And what was Ruth supposed to do, left alone for days at a time? She began to resent her daughter's enjoyment of other people's company.

At first of course it had been a pleasant novelty to have the house to herself, but very soon she started to miss Julie dreadfully, and the time came when Ruth began to complain about so many weekend activities, not to mention the camping trips.

'Why don't you give it a miss this year?' she'd suggest brightly, a pile of multi-coloured brochures at the ready. 'We could have a few days in Paris instead. Or Spain. What do you think?'

What Julie thought, especially as she got older, was that she had more fun scrambling to a chilly Elsan in the dead of night, or spying on the Scouts in the next field, than she ever had wandering around dusty cities with her mother. But Ruth was so insistent, offered so many tempting bribes, that gradually Julie's attendance at Brownies grew less and less frequent until by the time she was old enough for the Guides she'd lost the motivation altogether.

But as she leafed through the postcard stand in some icy gallery in Berlin or Amsterdam or Stockholm she would sometimes hear the little demon nagging at her shoulder.

'Is this really what you want to be doing? Eleven years old and following your Mum around boring museums?'

It prodded her painfully with a bony finger.

'You should be out with your friends, swopping secrets on the swings!'

It was right, of course.

Then it would pester Ruth, surfacing always at a time when she thought she was happy.

'Paris in the springtime, how romantic! But what's this? A little kid? You should be here with a handsome and princely lover,

126

taking off each other's clothes very very slowly through a long champagne afternoon. Holding hands across the table at a pavement cafe. Paris is for love...'

Yes, maybe so, thought Ruth. But that's easier said than done...

It was this very demon who one day persuaded Ruth to visit a reader of tarot cards.

It appeared one night when Julie was asleep in bed and Ruth was sitting in the stillness of the house listening to the sounds of people walking home from the pub down the road.

'Haven't you got any boyfriends?' the demon hissed in her ear.

She thought of Alex's knives and shook her head, but the demon persisted.

'They can't all be like him you know. Anyway...'

It drew closer still until it was right inside her brain.

'...what will you do when she leaves home? It's not long to go now, is it? And then what?'

'I must confess,' she thought, 'I am curious to know that else might happen in my life.'

She got up and went over to the mirror.

'You're not so bad-looking really,' she said to herself. 'Maybe it would be nice to get out into the world again.'

Idly, she picked up the local paper to fold it away, and then she saw

REBECCA ARMSTRONG — YOUR FUTURE IN THE CARDS

The next day she phoned for an appointment.

Ruth had never had her fortune read before. She felt rather silly as she drove out of town towards a village which in the last ten years had been transformed into a dormer development servicing various anonymous industrial estates.

Entering the outskirts of the swollen village she drove along shiny new roads past red-brick townhouses with wood-framed windows. Every house had a glaring patch of green lawn flanked by white alyssum, scarlet salvia, and a few bare-stemmed juvenile shrubs.

Through the upper windows of each home could be seen a brightly-coloured Dick Bruna baby mobile. Mothercare ride-on plastic tractors lay upturned in the drives, and inside the front windows the TV flashed playschool colours to a one-year old, a three-year old, and a twenty-five year old in Next jeans and a food-stained T-shirt.

The mid-morning communities of Meadow Way and Willow Mead hung deadly silent and double-glazed.

Then suddenly the road roughened into elderly pock-marks and soon Ruth found herself driving into the centre of the old village. She stopped to ask directions and found that Rebecca Armstrong lived in a row of post-war council houses just beyond the old Norman church.

Most of the gardens here were of the type Ruth desperately envied. Tidy rows of spuds, cabbage, carrots, onions — and not a weed in sight. In each one an elderly gardener stood sentinel with a sharpened hoe lest the smallest shoot of chickweed should venture above the surface of the soil.

But the third plot along made chaotic contrast to the others. If ever there was a potato here it had long disappeared beneath a carpet of couch grass and ground elder. Two ancient apple trees clawed at each other across an overgrown concrete path, and the wooden gate hung skew-whiff against a scrambling privet hedge.

Feeling ever more ridiculous but determined to go through with it, Ruth stepped over the fallen apples and rapped against the dirty glass of the front door. A woman opened it immediately.

'Er — Rebecca Armstrong? I've got an appointment. Eleven o'clock?'

'Yes alright duck. You're expected. Just come through and sit down in here for a moment, will you?'

The woman led the way into the barest living room Ruth had ever seen. The floor was covered with marbled black linoleum, cold and sticky and littered with bits of paper and cigarette butts. The only furniture in the entire room was a torn plastic settee which gave an airy sigh as she politely sank down in to it.

'It's a bit messy in here at the moment, duck,' said the woman. She laughed.

'Haven't got round to doing any cleaning yet this week.'

'There's more than a week's worth here,' thought Ruth distastefully as she tried not to look at the stained wall-paper. She consoled herself with the thought that whatever her future might hold, it certainly would never involve a place like this.

'Won't be a moment,' said Rebecca, and disappeared into the bowels of the house. Ruth wondered whether to make a break for it and leave before she caught some exotic disease — the smell in the room was painting an unpleasantly sticky taste on her throat — but before she could move the woman called her.

'You can come through now, love. Into the kitchen.'

Was it possible it could be even dirtier in here? Bottles half-full of rancid milk, chip wrappers, mouldy crusts. And flies rising in a cloud from something in a corner.

'I must be out of my mind,' she thought.

Rebecca had seated herself at a stained melamine kitchen table. Beckoning Ruth into the other chair, she swept away an old newspaper and laid down a pack of dog-eared tarot cards.

'Here's the money,' said Ruth. The table shook as she leaned over to lay down a ten pound note.

'Thanks duck. Now, just shuffle these for me, will you?'

Rebecca lit a cigarette and watched the movement of the cards in her client's hands.

'Is that enough?' Ruth handed them back, surreptitiously wiping her fingers on the side of her skirt.

'That'll do.' said the woman.

Then she began to talk. Ruth had intended to ask questions but it was difficult to interrupt the stream of information flowing from the woman as she leafed through the pack, laying out what seemed like random groups of cards.

'You've been lonely.'

'Well, I...'

'You've been very lonely, and you should be careful because it does strange things to your mind.'

She gazed at her client.

'It's not good for you to be on your own. It's OK for some people, but not for you.'

'Oh? Why...'

'Who's Julie?'

Ruth started.

'Julie. She's my daughter...'

'She's a fly one. She'll do something you don't expect. You want to watch her. Is she a good girl?'

'Oh yes...'

'She'll have a secret. She'll never tell you. I can see you in a boat.'

'We went to Venice last year...'

'You're on a boat and you're very happy, but you'll find you're wrong. You've already made one big mistake haven't you? Are you married?'

'Divorced.'

129

'That's not it. It's something else. But whatever it was, it's behind you now. You're ready for a change, aren't you? You've been biding your time, but now you've got to grow up.'

She banged the rickety table with a laugh, making Ruth jump.

'It's time you grew up, duck! You've got to get out into that big wide world — because if you don't...'

Rebecca threw down three more cards and became very serious.

'Look at these,' she said. 'If you're not careful you'll go wrong again. Listen. Here's The Chariot. You've already made one choice — and the Seven of Cups here says it was a mistake. That's the one I was telling you about. You've been wearing a mask, and it's too tight. It's hurting you, and it's hurting the people around you. Let me see your hand.'

The woman's fingers were warm and dry as she ran them over Ruth's palm.

'Mmm. You won't get the chance to put things right for a while, and when you do get it, I'm not even sure if you'll take it. Now look at this. This is The Moon. This is very, very important.'

She kept hold of Ruth's hand and patted it gently.

'Very, very important. Now, I'm going to explain it all so that when the time comes you'll understand how to handle it. But you'll have to be strong. It's up to you what you do.'

She held up the card and described it carefully.

'Look, at the bottom there's a deep pool of water, and there's a crayfish trying to climb out onto dry land. That's the part of you which you've got to fight. It's your unconscious, your imagination... do you understand what I mean?'

Ruth hesitated.

'I think so...'

'If you follow that, you'll fail. This animal, and the dogs you can see here, they belong to Hecate who guards the Gates of Hades. Now then, people used to believe that the dead passed through the Gates of Hades and then they were drawn up to the moon.'

'It's very beautiful,' said Ruth, gazing at the cool white beams of lunar light.

'Yeah. It is, isn't it? But it's not the way to go, not when you're still alive in this world.'

For heaven's sake, thought Ruth, does the woman think she's starring in a B-movie?

'Now look, can you see? There's a path. It's very narrow and dark, but you've got to try and follow it. If you don't keep your feet on that path you'll be pulled upwards to the moon before your time has come.'

Rebecca paused dramatically.

'That's when fantasy takes the place of reality,' she added in a stage whisper, filling Ruth with an overwhelming desire to giggle.

The woman put down the cards.

'Do you understand?' she asked.

'Uh, I'm not sure.'

'It means you'll be tempted to retreat into your imagination. But if you do that, you may never be able to get back onto the path.'

'Where does it lead?' Ruth was curious. She might as well play the woman along.

'To The Sun, my love. To new beginnings. And that's what you've got to aim for.'

'I'm sorry, but I really don't see how it applies to me. It doesn't make any sense.' replied Ruth. This was all complete mumbo-jumbo. What a waste of ten quid.

'Well, it will one day.'

'But I don't see what it is I'm supposed to do.'

'Can't help you there, duck. You'll have to come and see me again when the time comes.'

Rebecca pushed back her chair, indicating that the conversation was at an end. 'I hope you've enjoyed your reading,' she said with a tone of finality, as if the ten pounds in her psychic meter had just run out.

'But — can I just ask you — is there a man in there anywhere?' Now Ruth felt really silly. She had hoped someone would turn up in the cards without her having to ask.

'Not yet, my love. Come and see me again in a year's time and we'll have another look.'

Of course Ruth didn't go back.

She drove home that day feeling very foolish at having wasted so much money. The woman was a complete fraud — she didn't say anything of use at all. OK — she'd picked up Julie's name, but the character description was completely wrong. Julie had never been secretive — quite the opposite in fact. She never stopped chattering.

And all this stuff about the moon and climbing out of a pool and the Gates of Hades.

Utter nonsense.

131

Suddenly, abruptly, the bedroom is brightened by a shaft of white light falling through the window from the sullen clouds outside. The beam falls upon the sleeping Ruth, and in her dream she feels a chill.

It is unwise to tell fortunes backwards.

Downstairs, the house is silent with night. The back door still hangs open, admitting a dark breeze which flutters along the carpet to the sitting-room where the fire lies reduced to a mass of pale embers. It hardly warms the dog asleep on the hearth.

For want of anywhere else to go, the hens had returned when dusk fell and now they roost in rows along the back of the settee; on the piano; clinging to the bookshelves. They shuffle and mutter in their egg-dreams.

The window curtains hang back to reveal the swollen river as it slips away, pulling back to a distant sea.

This is not useful water. It is extra, surplus to requirements. What little life it contains it has squeezed and smashed with its own body, and beneath the currents the river bed lies churned and disfigured. If this water were a conscious being — and who is to say that it is not — it might be quivering in the exhausted aftermath of a temper tantrum.

In fact, this flood is the result of a meeting between a torrential downpour filling the rivers and a tidal downstream surge pushing them to over-flowing. It is a rarity, a coincidence, a fluke.

When was the last time you encountered water?

Of course, you may very well have prepared yourself a drink before settling down to read this book.

What have you got?

Tea, coffee, fizzy pop, gin and tonic? White wine, red wine, beer? Or maybe you prefer your water plain.

Is it hot or cold?

And how do you drink it?

Are you a slurper?

Or are you genteel?

When babies drink at the breast they open their throats and the milk simply runs down in huge swallows. They can breathe through their noses as they suck so there's no need to loosen the vacuum fix of their gums around the nipple.

Some children use this fluid caress of the gullet as a comforter, and even when they progress to drinking from a beaker they still gulp down the contents at speed, tipping the cup and pouring it down in a stream.

'Slow down! Slow down!' we say, gently pulling away the cup and teaching them to sip.

But sipping is a different pleasure.

A sip is a more restrained fluid-experience. We savour the texture of the drink, its heat or its chill, rolling it around our gums and tongue, swilling it across our back teeth, pushing it up against the roofs of our mouths. Cautiously we take care not to scald ourselves. We are tentative and slow. A sip is like a gentle kiss.

But if that is so then a gulp is a fellatial joy. There is no hesitancy about whether you will admit this liquid to your body. It hurtles in, engulfing your mouth for just a second before rushing into your throat and hitting the gullet with a smack. You feel it at the back, at the furthest point of sensation before the nerve-endings fade out and give way to the physically-unconscious interior of your body. You can hear the convulsion of your throat inside your ear as the fluid muscles its way down.

The mouth is where water is most vital to us, be it the gulp of colostrum after birth or the moistened sponge against the lips before death.

Do fish drink?

As a rule, fish in the sea drink a lot whereas those in freshwater drink very little. This is because the freshwater fish absorbs a great deal of fluid through its skin by the process of osmosis, but in saltwater species the process is reversed and water continually being lost through the gill membranes must be recouped by drinking.

The majority of human body-matter is water. We are droplets held together by the tension of heavier material, and at every moment we lose some water and replace it with more.

Blow against a mirror and you will see the fluid from inside your body as it re-materialises against the glass.

Examine it.

Those few drops have been everywhere.

A single molecule of water lying on that chill glass has been travelling the earth since the conception of our atmosphere (and perhaps before) because water is the very blood of our planet. Using our rivers for veins and our seas for arteries it endlessly circles through the flesh of the world renewing itself in a multitude of forms.

Recently it was hidden inside the gas of your own breath. Before then you drank it in a cup of herb tea, thinking you were doing yourself good for once.

But that water with which you filled the kettle has already made this journey through several bodies, and through a reasonably efficient purification system (you hope).

Prior to that, it fell from the sky into a mountain reservoir. It came from a cloud, which was born above a desert as the fluids evaporated from the carcass of a diseased camel lying abandoned in the sand.

Or maybe the sun sucked it up from an ice-floe in Antarctica, licking snow mountains like ice-lollies.

Water is a sensitive organ, highly responsive to its environment. Simple agitation of a glass of water can bring about measurable molecular changes, and we are all familiar with the way that a stone cast into a pond will send ripples across the whole mass.

Some scientists even believe that it undergoes a cycle of growth, decay, and renewal. They even say that interfering with this process may have harmful effects to the body of the planet. For example, water brought from deep underground may be 'unripe', whilst by the same token recycled and many-times purified city water may have been refined until it is no longer living.

Now you have a molecule of water on your mirror. What will you do with it? Why not wipe it against your sleeve? It is hardly damp after all. It will disappear quickly into the air and may be caught by the leaves of that dried-out philodendron on the window-sill.

And there are other ways of course.

You could have chosen not to exhale your molecule, but to sweat it out in a salty cocktail spiked with urea.

Or you could keep hold of it for a while, mixing it in your saliva and making it work for you. Perhaps it could help you digest a cheese sandwich, following it down to your stomach and blending with the intestinal juices.

You may like to contribute it to your blood, where it could do life-

134

saving work by running around at speed energizing and feeding your tissues. But mind you don't cut yourself with that cheese knife — oh! — too late

Ouch, that hurt didn't it? Now, if it hasn't escaped through the cut, it's probably leaving through your eyes and runny nose as you cry with the pain. (I'll wait while you get an elastoplast.)

It's hard to keep hold of.

Water.

If it hasn't gone already it will manage to depart in your urine or your menstrual blood or your seminal fluid.

Oh, so many ways.

We have established that today you have already encountered water by:

— drinking it

— urinating it

— salivating it

— and sweating it.

At the very least.

What else?

Well, no doubt you washed this morning?

Did you have a soaky bath? An invigorating shower? Or just a lick and a promise at the wash-basin? Perhaps you performed your ablutions beside a clear cold mountain stream, you lucky person.

No doubt you used soap, and later you squeezed detergent to wash up your crockery. And more again in the washing machine. I don't need to tell you where all those chemicals went to afterwards.

We grow our vegetables with water; wash them in water; cook them in water.

We walk in the rain.

We play in the snow.

We slip on the ice.

And we swim!

Oh, how we love to swim! Leaping between the waves and cruising the shallows with snorkels and scuba tanks. We paddle about in boats, trailing a hand in the swell.

Humans love to pretend they're fish. Or seals. Or dolphins or whales.

We float, buoyed up by the salt, fearing the nip of sand-buried crabs.

We dive into lakes and rivers to feel the cool smoothness of fresh water on our thirsty skins.

We pay money to take off our clothes in the airless talcummed atmosphere of the leisure centre and plunge into the diluted waste products of a thousand other people, and then we praise ourselves for being so healthy.

Julie,
however,
hated
swimming.

Although Ruth had nothing but scorn for the tarot reader and her chaotic home, she found that she could not get The Moon out of her head.

The deep pool began to exert a powerful influence on her subconscious. Sometimes she had dreams about it, and she would wake up feeling as if she were bursting through into the air. She was gasping for breath. Her face would feel wet, but it was only tears.

She could find no reason for it.

On making an impulse decision to go to the swimming pool more often, she did not remember the dreams which had led her there, and she made no connection between her visits and the subsequent restful sleep.

In fact, without realising it she was subjecting herself to the soothing effects of the dive reflex. The minute she felt the touch of water on her cheeks her pulse rate dropped from seventy to thirty beats a minute. She didn't know it, but she was returning to her beginnings. To our beginnings. To life before the land. The source.

A powerful and dedicated swimmer, she would pound up and down for forty lengths without a stop then climb out, shower and dress, and go to wait on the steps outside until her daughter finally shambled out dragging a soggy plastic bag and sucking a Mars bar.

Julie knew how to swim. She could haul her body along the water for a few lengths when required. But she hated putting her head under, and she swam a clumsy breast-stroke with her neck stretched above the slip-stream until her spine and shoulders began to ache. As she faltered in the lane nearest the edge she kept a constant lookout for divers who might splash, or bellyfloppers likely to deluge her with spray. Every now and then Ruth would course by at speed, her blind head rearing sideways out of the water, her legs kicking with fast controlled power.

When Julie was smaller she had liked best to play games in the shallow end. She loved to cling to her mother's neck in the drenching intimacy of slippery wet flesh. Ruth was gentle with her daughter then. She calmed the fear away and let Julie ride on her back as she schoonered round the pool. The child wallowed in the contact, the heat of her mother's body emanating through her cool skin, and she would bury her head in Ruth's damp curls and breathe in her perfume.

But Ruth's patience had a purpose. It was intended to persuade Julie to swim alone and unaided, thus liberating her mother to run away to the deep end and plunge like a submarine into the white-lined depths. Julie's first swimming certificate became the badge of Ruth's watery independence, and soon she found herself playing on her own again near the ladder while Ruth threshed up and down the pool keeping her nightmares at bay.

Julie would kneel tentatively in the shallows until the water reached her shoulders, and pretend she was swimming. If anyone came near she twitched and blinked at the slightest splash, wheeling round to check the proximity of the edge.

There were unpleasant things on the bottom of the pool too. She could feel someone else's elastoplast drifting against her toe; a piece of grit caught her foot; tiny soggy clumps of tissue — human and paper — floated by in the murk. She saw people blowing their noses into their fingers and spitting into the water, and yellow streams of urine issuing from between the legs of innocent-faced swimmers.

Then something would suddenly clutch at her legs and she would jump with horror to find a long pink shape circling her like a shark. It was Ruth, popping up out of the bath of human detritus, dripping with smiles and urging her to follow.

She shook her head.

Julie hated swimming pools.

When she was twelve she was relieved to be considered old enough to stay at home alone while Ruth visited the pool, coming home bathed in that familiar stench of changing rooms which caught Julie's throat and made her want to vomit.

But despite her regular visits Ruth found the public pool only partially satisfying. She'd get a good night's sleep afterwards, but she was aware that it was only an incomplete experience. In the summer months she preferred to swim in a nearby lake. Preferable, but still not perfect.

In the evening of a long hot day the lake was deserted. Green weed trailed from her ankles as she emerged from the cool water under a fading blue sky fringed with weeping willows.

Moorhens flew overhead.

Tench and pike swam below.

In the distance a lone sailboarder cruised slowly against a green backdrop, the striped sail arrowing in the direction of a white sliver of early moon.

And then, of course, there was the possibility of ocean.

If the Moon card had reminded Ruth of anything, it was the sea.

It had long been a frustration for her to live so far inland, and when in spring the seagulls quitted the city for the coast she would get out her maps and start to plan.

She spent hours with her guide-books and hotel brochures spread out across the kitchen table, ever searching for the ultimate seaside holiday, and as the weeks went by and summer approached she became increasingly oppressed by her land-locked home.

At first she had planned to change jobs, to move closer to the edges of the land, but work was scarce and she was trapped by her specialisation. What else could a middle-aged historian do if not teach? So she resigned herself to the prospect of a retirement cottage by the sea. She would get there eventually. But meanwhile the annual holidays kept her going.

Then sometimes too, they travelled abroad to dusty cities where Julie muttered and complained while Ruth pinned culture around her daughter like an ill-fitting dress.

After the cities, the seasides were meant to be a concession. Ruth believed that all kids love the sea-side, but although this conviction suited her mother, who adored a bucket-and-spade holiday, Julie was of a different opinion.

The promenades were okay. And shops and arcades. Funfairs, open-topped buses...

At the sea-side Julie spent and spent. Copper after copper slid into shining machines and sticks of rock slipped down the throat. Another go on the dodgems. One more ride on the waltzer.

Anything, anything, to keep away from the beach.

On the beach you could drown in sand, suffocate in the sea, be blown off the rocks.

Danger danger.

Red flags and life-boats.
Life-jackets.
Life-guards.
Life-saving equipment for every eventuality.
Was the sea trying to tell her something?
So she shook out her towels and sat upright, gritting her teeth as she watched her only parent, her single parent, bobbing in the surf and hurling herself between the waves. How irresponsible. What if she drowned and never came back? What if the tide turned and carried her away?

Then there she was in the distance, wading into pools and stumbling amongst the barnacled rocks. Broken legs. Concussion. Poison. Pollution.

Because it is so highly responsive to its environment, water has been described as a sensitive organ. Indeed, the simple agitation of a glass of water can bring about measurable molecular changes, and we're all familiar with the way that a stone cast into a pond will send ripples across the whole mass.

Some scientists even believe that, like us, water undergoes a cycle of growth and decay, but that unlike us it has the power to renew itself. It's certainly true that the quantity of water on the earth has remained constant since our planet was born, and it therefore makes sense that water should be left alone to follow its own path through the cycle, especially because any interference with this process may have harmful effects to the body of the planet.

For example, water brought from deep underground may be 'unripe', whilst by the same token recycled and many-times purified city water may have been refined until it is so depleted it could be literally described as dead.

We must ask ourselves whether we are repurifying the world's stock of water to such an extent that it may soon no longer be capable of self-rejuvenation?

Is it possible for the planet to survive on dead water, which not only has no nutrients but more seriously has no spirit either?

Now, far out on the horizon there is no-one to save Ruth as she slowly submerges into Ruari. Despite all the power of her imaginings, his qualities remain essentially twin to those of his element and source — he is unstable, frictionless, soft yet unstoppably invasive. And she must not delude herself that he is any more human now than he was in the churchyard when they made their vows.

Every time they've made love he has flooded within her and voyaged through the very flesh and tissue of her body until now she is sodden with him, immersed and drowning in him, awash with his fluids of sex and sweat and salt. She is engulfed, submerged, and beyond rescue.

But her lover is like Crusoe in reverse. Increasingly he longs to get off the dry land where he has been marooned for so long. His flesh is already made scratched and sore by this parched abrasive country. He has never learned to survive except through the conjuring of Ruth's embraces and now, like the mistletoe which sucks the apple tree until it dies, so she has become overburdened with their passion and can no longer succour its weight.

Now, in her sleep, she wonders whether she was mistaken to make Ruari be so dangerously and untimely born, because nothing can hold water forever and whatever it touches will begin to dissolve until eventually, no matter how long it takes, the container and the contained will become one.

Part Four

T'ien Hou

According to Chinese mythology T'ien Hou was a girl on the island of Mei-chou, and she had four brothers who were all sailors on different ships.

One day when her brothers were away at sea, T'ien Hou fainted and fell into a coma. For a while everyone thought she was dead, but with the aid of many powerful stimulants she came back to life. However as soon as she regained consciousness she complained of a pressing conviction that she had been awakened too soon, but did not know why.

The reason became clear when three of her brothers returned to tell of how their ships had all fallen victim to a violent storm, but in the height of the tempest their sister had appeared to each one and saved them from danger.

Only the fourth brother perished — the girl had been revived before she had time to go to his aid.

Even after her death T'ien Hou continued helping sailors in peril and is known today as the Empress of Heaven and the protector of navigators.

Simon takes out his wallet and extracts two photographs.

In the first, a toddler sits naked in a green plastic paddling pool. She is emptying a yoghurt pot full of water over her head, her mouth wide open with delight. Whenever he looks at that photo he can hear her joyous yells, and then she says 'Da-Da!'. But over the years the words have come in his mind to resemble the hollow cackle of a talking doll, and these days he pulls the string of memory less and less.

The voice of the other photograph is one he has never heard. The picture is carefully posed and out of it stare the anxious eyes of a young woman. She wears make-up, carefully applied, and her hair is cut short in an angular fashion. Every strand is in place. Small silver earrings and just the top edge of a buttercup yellow sweater. On the reverse of the photo there is a small sticker which says 'Stein & Co. Photographs for that Special Occasion.'

The voice belonging to the picture has spoken to him twice in recent weeks, both times through the medium of paper. It has made great attempts to control its spidery hand-writing and every missive begins neatly and with a regular slope to the left, but by the middle of the first page it starts to wobble until the letter ends with a messy flourish of words tumbling over the page in a waterfall of detail. He reflects, as he turns the photos between his fingers, that she has told him a lot about herself with her emotional calligraphy, but soon he will hear her voice for real.

In fact, at this very moment a silver car is hesitating to a stop in the street outside, and he knows it must be her. He fights a sudden desire to slip out of the back door and disappear before she can knock, but his feet betray him and carry him forward, down the neat path and through the wrought-iron gate, and his voice is calling 'Hello Darling!'

She is still sitting behind the wheel, and she too is regretting this meeting before it has even begun. She is about to restart the engine and drive away when she hears his voice and accepts that there is no going back. She steps out of the car and faces him.

'Hello Dad.'

He has prepared a treat.

A welcome party.

After unloading her case and depositing it inside the featureless front hall, he leads her straight down to the harbour.

'We'll have something once we're on board,' he says as he hustles her down the cobbled streets. 'We've got to catch the afternoon tide, and then we'll talk, eh?'

He smiles at her quickly and nervously, but she is staring straight ahead at the small bay in front of them.

'Where are we going?'

'The Mimi, of course. I sent you a photo didn't I? Yes, I'm sure I did.'

He's gabbling now, the words tangling themselves in his mouth, and it has not occurred to him that she might not wish to sail in his beloved boat.

It is necessary that he confronts this situation with the rolling sea beneath his feet. He has never been too confident on land — too many solid obstacles — but on board the Mimi he feels secure. She is his own floating reef, Prospero's island, his private dominion.

For many years the Bank has been his anchor. When his marriage to Ruth went sour and he wanted to untie his moorings and flee, it was happy to arrange a transfer so that he could make a new life for himself and Jeannette. He left his first family behind to make a new one, but there was never a child. Then suddenly, after so many years of happiness, his second wife found that the guilt permanently resident inside her — fed by remorse at having deprived Ruth and Julie of a husband and father — had hardened itself into a fast-growing brain tumour. By then, after several transfers around the country, Simon had been consigned to this remote back-water, manager of the only branch in a tiny fishing community. Twelve months later, after sliding into the solitary world of the blind, Jeannette had finally passed away leaving her grieving husband alone for the first time in his life.

After her death he bought the Mimi. He and Jeannette had always promised themselves a boat, and now at last they had one. As he fiddled amateurishly with the engine he would chatter to his wife and keep her informed of its progress.

But he remained unbearably, desperately lonely.

Without Jeannette to navigate his way through daily life Simon has become vulnerable, and still cannot deal with the dangerous currents caused by people and their emotions. Perhaps, he thinks hopefully, now that my grown-up daughter is here she'll take care

142

of me as Jeannette used to.

Meanwhile Julie, who has been afraid of water all her life, stands beside the Mimi which tips and bucks in the gentlest of swells as her father leaps aboard and unties the ropes. Has she come this far only to be engulfed? She considers refusing to go with him, but there's no way she can turn back now.

'Come on!' he shouts excitedly, comfortable now that his feet are solid on the deck. 'All aboard!'

She takes a deep breath and steps off dry land.

Simon has brought beer, sandwiches, fruit and cake, and Julie is surprised to find she can eat the feast without feeling queasy.

This is the first time he has entertained company aboard the Mimi — with the exception, of course, of the spectral Jeannette.

As they make their way across the harbour and out to sea he tells her about Scotland, about the Bank, and of course the boat. She listens politely to his meticulous instructions on how best to sail the Mimi and reflects to herself that he seems much more ordinary than she remembers — but then she remembers very little. The father she has grown in her imagination is very different from this rather boring and dowdy man with his ship-shape habits and sharp moustache. He should be a heartless villain, a deserter, a dangerous criminal. But he's none of these things.

He's a chatterer. He's hardly stopped talking since they left the bay. And always about himself. He yatters on self-importantly, his tight little face twitching as he accurately recalls every little detail of whichever tedious tale he is relating at the moment.

Julie fades in and out of the conversation like a ghost, and wonders what her mother had ever seen in him.

As the wind flaps noisily in the sails and Simon fusses with the jib — 'Duck when I give the word!' — she huddles furiously in her orange flotation jacket and regrets she ever came.

As soon as they get back to shore she will make her excuses and leave.

She had not known what to expect of this reunion — sobs, tension, guilt, recriminations — maybe just a relaxed and friendly meeting as if they had never been apart — but not this blithe egocentric prattle. At the very least he could have held her tight and begged forgiveness...

'Of course,' Simon is saying, 'the wildlife along this coast is

143

extremely varied, so obviously you need a good pair of binoculars. I got these...' he points to the glasses hanging around his scrawny neck '...from the chandlers on the quay. Harris's. You may have noticed it as you drove in — little white building — rather scruffy — anyway, I was very lucky because I'd just thought to myself what you need my boy, I thought, what you need is a damn good pair of binoculars. You've got to get the best. And I just wandered down to the shop one day, a Saturday morning I think it was, about half past ten, and there they were in the window. Twenty pounds off! Well, I went straight in and...'

'Dad?'

He stops in full flow, still fingering the smooth black safety cord of the bargain price binoculars.

It feels strange to be called Dad again after all these years.

Julie grips the side of the boat as the sea rises to rinse her fingers with salt.

"I was just wondering... how did you and Mum get together? You seem so... so... different...'

'Ah...'

He runs his thumb along his pale chin. The hours he spends on the sea have failed to raise colour in his greying complexion.

'Yes, well, we were very different. That's why I — we — split up, you see...'

'But how did you first meet?'

She obviously isn't going to give up. He realises he'll have to answer the question before he can finish the story of the binoculars.

'Just a moment — watch out!'

Swinging the jib gives him a little more time. The evening breeze is starting to build up and they should be heading back. He fusses with assorted ropes then sits down again.

'Well, I was working at the bank — assistant manager even then — only twenty-five — rapid promotion — doing very well, actually — anyway your mother was a student — used to come in to plead for an overdraft — terrible with money — well, I asked her out. She was pretty, and she brought a breath of fresh air into the office. So I took her to dinner — little Chinese place — bloke had an account with us — he was doing very well, as a matter of fact — I seem to remember he was planning to expand at the time, and I'd promised the boss I'd give the place a look over — very promising... anyway, we got on well together, and after a while I asked her to marry me.'

'But didn't she go out with — you know — she must have had friends at college. I mean, I wouldn't have thought...'

'She was a bit of a loner, your mother. Probably still is. And those other students — very immature. Drinking, taking drugs. Whereas — look at me! I could offer her security you see. But...'

He pauses as if, after all these years, a revelation has suddenly hit him,

'...but I hadn't really expected her to go back after we married. It never occurred to me that she'd actually want to *work*.'

He pronounces this last word carefully, as if it was the key to all his troubles, then his face hardens as the stream of memory begins to flow...

'I thought she was just studying to fill in the time until she got married. But then they offered her some part-time teaching and she took it. Even though you were only a baby! After that I'd get home from the office and the place would be a tip — an absolute tip! — she'd been reading all day - would you believe it! Research, she called it, for her precious Ph.D., but as far as I could see it was just an excuse to slop about doing nothing. There you'd be, upstairs crying in your cot while she was fast asleep on the settee under a pile of books — and no dinner cooked either...'

He shudders at this uncharacteristic escape of anger and feels around his chest to check the straps of his buoyancy aid.

'I'll tell you what she was! She was a dreamer. A dreamer!!'

Julie trails her hand in the water and is silent.

'Whereas, Jeannette... she worked on Direct Debits — beautiful handwriting — head for figures. She... well, she suited me better.'

This is the time, thinks Julie, when I ask him why he sent back my letters. Slowly, she is filling up with fury. There was no need to desert me, just because he couldn't live with her. True, he never failed to credit their bank account with the proper amount of maintenance every month but — she clenches her teeth — surely he knows other currencies than money?

But she does not really need to ask. She has now been in the company of her father for almost three hours, and the answer is devastatingly clear. She feels very calm, because now she knows the truth. He's not a criminal, not a serious malefactor, he's not even a reasonably nice man. He's just a waste of time, she tells herself, a bloody stupid waste of time.

My God, she remembers, Mum always said that they were better off without him, but Julie had thought she was being brave. No! She wasn't! She was damned right.

145

There's only one important person in Simon's life — himself.

She feels fleetingly sorry for Jeannette, unable to imagine her father nursing a sick woman with his endless mindless prattle. No wonder her brain exploded, she thinks cruelly.

Confident that he has answered her question in full and without reservation, Simon prepares to continue the story of the purchase of the incredibly cheap binoculars when the ribbed back of a huge basking shark surfaces nearby.

Julie, searching in the other direction for sight of the coast, does not see the fish and so is only aware of her father's horrified scream before the vessel capsizes and she is underwater fighting for air.

Upon noticing the monster Simon had leapt to his feet in terror.

The boat, badly rigged by a novice sailor too busy showing off to do his job properly, had immediately capsized and thrown them both headlong into the sea just above Beaufort's Dyke.

Beaufort's Dyke. You can find it on a navigational map of Britain's coastal waters. Four miles off-shore and three hundred and fifteen metres deep, it made a useful dumping ground for the country's bad memories after World War II. The deepest part of the Irish Sea, and a resting place for huge supplies of unwanted munitions. Almost a quarter of a mile below Julie's flailing body lies a soldier's graveyard of tanks, lorries, guns and ammunition, all rusting in Davy Jones's Locker.

Meanwhile, the basking shark, second biggest fish in the world — the whale shark beats it by several tons — plunges under the waves and sniffs them from below. Its highly pressure-sensitive body detects Julie's every movement as she thrashes towards the overturned dinghy.

Cetorhinus Maximus is unusual amongst its predatory species in that it eats only plankton. This particular specimen is of average size, about twenty-five feet long and weighing only a few tons, and its fearsome aspect gives no clue to its preferred diet. In fact, its bulk makes it so slow moving that it is a popular prey for local fishermen who know it as a lucrative and safe target.

Now it's true that Simon owns a fully comprehensive recently revised guide to the fishes of the Northern oceans, but the book is so complicated he has not yet finished reading it. If he had, he would have known that the appearance, only yards from the boat, of a twenty-five foot basking shark is no real cause for alarm.

But it's too late for that.

The shark sniffs them, rejects them, and moves off towards a deliciously-scented cloud of tiny fish some distance away, leaving Julie and Simon bobbing among the waves in their fancy state-of-the-art life-jackets.

Recovering from the cold shock of submersion, Julie propels herself towards her father who floats a few yards away, his head slumped in the water.

He is unconscious but breathing.

Holding his face above the swell she strikes out for the Mimi and by grasping a loosened rope manages to tie him against the fibre-glass hull.

She tries to gather her thoughts whilst continuing to support Simon's head above the water line. Although she is gently kicking her feet all the time to keep her circulation going there is a sinister chill spreading through her limbs, and she realises that for her father to have any chance of recovery she must ward off hypothermia by huddling herself against him.

She cuddles close against his torso, supporting his head on her shoulder as if she were burping a baby, and as his limbs knock limply against hers she searches the horizon.

Meanwhile, in the house above the flood Ruari can feel his consciousness slipping from liquid to solid and back again as he allows himself to be reshaped. He becomes a flowing jellyfish skimming the skin of the sea with his miles and miles of tubular stinging tentacles.

Then, just as he is getting used to this fluid and massive form his flesh begins to shiver and he is sucked out, evaporated into the waiting air and rising molecule by molecule into the dusty wind, twisting and threshing against sharp particles of sand, carried forcefully away from the sea and towards a group of towering golden cliffs which conceal a forest folded away behind their backs.

He can feel the hot exhaled breath of the trees far below as he is enfolded by clouds and comes to rest for a moment inside their dull whiteness.

There is a pause. Distantly, he can detect the tense drawing thirst of the forest below, until suddenly the air contorts in a huge spasm and he is scattered downwards once more. Down he rushes, at a thousand miles an hour, down to the parched and waiting trees, and with the first touch of cool leaves he remembers from

147

somewhere the faint smell of skin and two lips so wet he had almost dissolved in their kisses... *I am poured out like water, and all my bones are out of joint...* and then magically she is in front of him and a human form has once more gathered itself around his shifting, unstable shape.

And once again, as so many times before, he is watching her sleep.

But reaching out to caress her, he finds that his flesh is no longer fixed enough to conjoin with hers — instead, his fading fingers leave only the wet streaks of tear-stains on her cheeks. There will be no more touching here. No more the pleasures of loving, or moaning, or sighing. No more lips, no more tongues, no more damp embraces. She can hardly feel him, and makes no response. It's almost as if he no longer exists...

He moves once more to the window where the yellow shirt still hangs on the sill, a signal pleading for rescue. Below, the grey river sweeps on. In a vision, he suddenly believes that somewhere out there is a bottomless lake inhabited by creatures of glowing phosphorescence, and even as his desire for it comes upon him, his mortal form begins once more to collapse in on itself and to break up. But... *my heart also in the midst of my body is even like melting wax...* and he is brought back again by the memory of their first visit to the lake which even now lies buried beneath the flood.

He remembers putting his hands on her shoulders and entering her quickly whilst pushing her down hard, down under the water, until she was fully submerged. As she panicked and struggled to breathe he had been filled with terror and was about to pull her upwards to the air when suddenly she'd opened her eyes and smiled. At last, there in his true element, she was witnessing the proper nature of this being she believed she'd invented, but who in fact has always existed somewhere between the water world and the solid.

As he hovered shimmering and changing before her he was filled with the sensuous ecstasy of being watched, his every fibre and every nerve tingling with rapture, and all the time her eyes had never wavered from an intensive and hungry gaze. With her look she consumed him as his skin began to glow with phosphor, and beneath her caress his flesh turned to soft aquamarine scales.

He had striven deeper within her as they drifted along the bed of the lake, and when her orgasm came she seemed momentarily

148

to melt into the water around them. Then suddenly he forgot his human form and cried out aloud as somewhere deep inside him a cell divided and the sperm of every fish pushed its way urgently through his flesh and into the body of the lake.

And at that moment he had lost her, left her floating there alone on the lake because he could for not for even a moment longer sustain his physical form. She had disappeared on one side of the barrier, he on the other, and it had been hours before he was able to struggle back again.

Now, he can barely even touch her and the transition is getting harder and harder to maintain. But there must be a way...

Climbing into bed he wraps himself around her body until every inch of her skin is wet with him, and then he covers her sleeping eyes with kisses. Pushing his tongue into the welcoming dampness of her lips, he laps at her saliva as he tries to drink her inside himself, and between his legs an erection begins to swell with the fluids of blood and sex.

At first, it had seemed she could barely feel him at all, but now she begins to stir beneath his caresses and again with his tongue he wets her lips as they curve into a sleepy smile. Her mouth is making the open vowels of his name and pouring them lovingly into his ear, and surely they will be together now?

It is hard to estimate distance at sea, but Julie guesses the coast must be several miles away.

The sun has gone down quickly. She can see lights beginning to twinkle in the villages and the splashes of car headlamps against the darkened shape of the land.

The last thing she remembers is Simon's screamed 'Look out!' before the Mimi tipped over and dropped them both into the ice-cold water, but she has no idea of the reason for his alarm. Now he's breathing noisily in her ear, his open mouth rattling out a confused morse code. Little balls of froth cling to his tidy moustache like birthday cake icing.

'There, there,' soothes Julie in her best baby voice.

She pats the back of his life-jacket and curses him under breath.

He has brought her to this — her worst nightmare come true — and now he's making her keep him alive.

She spits into the water and shifts her position uncomfortably.

It's hard to believe that she had just driven for three hundred miles only to finish up adrift in the Irish Sea in the dead of night accompanied by the very last person in the world she'd want to drown with.

She keeps nodding off to sleep but is constantly shaken awake again by Simon's body bumping against her.

Finally she senses a change in his weight and his legs begin a feeble kicking. She looks down, and sees his pale eyes opening. He seems to be coming round.

'Help me...'

'It's okay,' she says, fighting to stay afloat against his weak struggles.

'What happened...?' He's shivering violently, his teeth chattering out the words.

Just a minute, thinks Julie, he's my Dad. Shouldn't he be taking care of me?

Suddenly, exultantly, she realises that none of this matters. What's important is that she's got him. He's in her power. This is the man she has hated since even before she could read and write. Who ignored her childish drawings. Who never sent a birthday card. Who abandoned her to a crazy woman. Who never wrote. Never phoned.

They say that when you're drowning your whole life flashes past your eyes. It's just unfortunate for Simon that he's within striking distance when it happens to Julie.

'Now, class, I want everyone to draw a picture of their family. Put your daddy on this side, your mummy here, your sisters and brothers there...'

'Pupils are requested to bring both parents to the meeting...'

'Haven't you got a Dad then?...'

'He's run away...'

'Your Mum's weird. Why isn't she married?...'

'Who'll give you away on your wedding day Julie?...'

'No-one. Her Dad's given her away already hah hah hah!...'

She pulls him close, grasps his chin roughly, and stares into those watery eyes.

'Where were you, Dad?'

'Huh?' He feels sick. He's going to throw up. His stomach heaves and turns inside out and she's shouting in his ear as he vomits a bucketful of beer and sandwiches into the water.

150

'I said where were you? You left me, you bastard!'

They are swirling together in a whirlpool of debris, little gobbets of sick clinging to their clothes, and now she's screaming out there in the wide ocean where no-one can hear. She's screaming at the top of her voice.

'I was only a little kid! How could you do it!'

'Julie...' He can't understand what the fuss is about.

'Julie...'

She pauses, relieved. He's finally going to say it. He's going to apologise. He's going to make it right after all these years. He's summoning up his long-forgotten father's voice, he's drumming it up from the past, the voice which takes control of the situation and makes everything okay again. He's going to calmly apologise and then the lifeboat will arrive and we'll be rescued and...

'Julie...' he gasps as they spin together in the current, 'don't be so ridiculous...'

'WHAT?'

She's speechless with fury. How dare he?

Her arms are numb with cold but she heaves them up until her swollen hands are resting on his slippery balding scalp, then with all her strength she pushes him down under the waves.

'I'm seeing my Dad this weekend. When's yours coming Julie?'

Despite the shock of submersion he's still quite strong. He's trying to pull her off him and his nails are scratching deep into the back of her hands. There are streaks of her blood in the water. She raises a fist and hits him hard against the ear.

'Stop it!'

'Don't cry, love. He's probably just missed the last date for Christmas posting...'

'You bastard!'

Suddenly, like a cork out of a bottle, he pops up gasping for air. She has to use all her weight to push him under again, but she manages it by throwing her stomach on top of him as if he were a surfboard. He's going crazy, arms and legs flailing out in all directions beneath her. At this rate he'll pull her down too. He's trying to crawl up her body, grasping her leg and hauling himself up, but she won't let him.

'For tonight's homework, I'd like you all to interview your fathers and find out...'

She brings up her knee underwater as hard as she can and feels it connect with his chin. Another streak of blood floats up — probably from his bitten tongue.

She wants to smash his bones. She wants to rip out his stony incapable heart.

'You left us ALONE!'

The man in the water struggles for a second longer, then suddenly all falls still. A cloud of red bubbles bursts on to the surface of the sea.

'It's a lovely painting Julie, but haven't you missed someone out?...'

She lets go, and slowly he bobs up again. Pulling away to inspect him she studies his open mouth flecked with blood and his empty eyes. She's dreamt of seeing this face for so long, but really it was never much to look at.

Now here she is, adrift and alone in the cold night with a stranger who has never been a proper father and now is not anything.

She releases her hold and his body sinks gently until it comes to rest just below the waves. As his hollow mouth fills up like a jug, she allows herself one small smile. The lifeboat hasn't turned up yet, but she's rescued herself anyway, that's for sure.

His body is still tied to the rolling hull of the Mimi.

She remembers a scene from Moby Dick where Captain Ahab, in his final battle against the whale, lashes himself to the harpoon ropes around its vast body and continues to stab at it until it dives, fathoms and fathoms, and drowns him. When it surfaces again the sailors can see their dead commander still tied to the whale's enormous bulk, and the motion of the animal causes his free arm to swing to and fro in a ship-mate's greeting. His mortal enemy has now become his grave. A macabre and sinister sight, this beckoning arm waving from a drowned body.

Simon's corpse has no such dignity.

Now submerged for the last time, the lungs are filling with water, sending incoherent messages bubbles to the surface. His thinning hair floats like pale weed as he gently spins in the current.

Julie leaves him and eases herself round to the other side of the boat.

Her fingers are so numb now that she cannot grasp properly and it's almost a relief when her hand slips and she finds herself drifting away from the dinghy and its gruesome companion.

The sea has roughened and constantly swamps her face so that she must make a continual effort to breathe air.

But there is yet one face, and one face only, which keeps

recurring before her stinging eyes, and she hears herself calling out to it again and again...

Ruth, asleep in the flood, is trying to dream of mermaids but the dream won't come.

Instead, it's another dream of babies.

She's in a small harbour — an old fishing town — and there are families waiting on the sea-front.

The dream is black and white and grey. Grey for the sea and sky, black for the buildings, and white for the faces of the people who stand waiting.

In the bay the slate-coloured ocean shakes itself like a small wet dog, white strips of jagged surf riding along miniature waves, while some distance away rowing boats fight against the swell.

Ivory-skinned against the dark street, the families huddle in silent groups to watch the progress of the boats.

Ruth the dreamer floats invisible above them. She is an impartial observer kept aloft by the thick web of tension in the air.

Finally the first craft lands against the splintered jetty and the families move forward towards it.

One of the men in the boat stands up, shaking his head with regret as he cradles forth a baby girl, recently drowned. Of the waiting groups, two families come forward. They are driven to look, but they don't want to see.

As each couple peers into the sodden blanket a wife and husband exchange glances, nodding stiffly to the man. The other couple turn away.

The air is rigid with sorrow as the parents take their child, but at the same time they cannot help but query whether she's really theirs. Her face is blown with drowning — perhaps it isn't her after all — they can't fully recognize those underwater features.

They both think this question, but neither voices it.

The older children gather round and they all stare mutely at the closed and swollen water-logged eyes.

Then further down the shore another boat comes, and the waiting people surge towards it, pushing the childless couple before them. There have been two infants lost. Perhaps this one will have survived. Still holding their child the parents follow the group, clinging to the hope that there has been a mistake. Maybe the first baby will prove not to be theirs after all.

Ruth the dreamer floats above them towards the approaching boat, then she overtakes and reaches it just as the people turn their eyes to a second outstretched bundle and gasp aloud.

This is the first sound anyone has made above the moans of the sombre sea.

In the boatman's arms lies a wrapped bundle of chewed blue flesh. Only the face can be seen, and it is bitten and ragged, the wounds washed clean by salt but already blackening in the air. The eyes have gone, the nose only two dark holes, no lips around the toothless gums. The bereaved couple make no attempt to take the child, but turn away once again as the mother falls weeping into the arms of her silent children.

Ruth cannot stop staring at the fish-eaten face.

Is this what the sea does?

Her beloved waters?

At this moment the first couple arrive just in time to catch a glimpse of the child before it is wrapped over again, and seeing its horrific injuries they are filled with relief and guilt as they survey once more their own perfect corpse, knowing for certain she must belong to them.

As they hurry away Ruth is left alone to weep and her tears fall into the darkening sea below and wet the streets of the town.

Her sorrow is like endless rain. Her eyes are no sooner emptied than they fill up again with regret and shame because now she knows who those babies are and, worse, she knows who is responsible for their suffering.

Tossing in her sleep she feels a weight along the length of her limbs. It is the heavy shape of Ruari and his passion, but she is sunk so deep in sleep she has no knowledge of his presence and is absorbed only in her own moment. She knows now that she must act, and soon, because those babies are all Julie, and all Ruth as well. They have perished in the cruel sea for no other reason than Ruth's own renunciation of them.

Suddenly the Tarot reader's card for the Moon flashes into her mind. But now it brings with it another woman, not from the Arcana but from Greek mythology.

Selene.

Selene who every evening rises into the sky to illuminate the shadowy night with her golden crown, and who once stole a kiss from the beautiful human Endymion as he lay sleeping. He, hoping to make her love him forever, asked Zeus for immortality and eternal youth and was granted these on one condition — that he

154

remained eternally and forever asleep. And so it is that the golden Selene comes every night to watch over her lover as the rays of the amorous moon caress the sleep of mortals.

Endymion chose permanent unconsciousness as the price of joy, and as a result gained no joy at all since he was never awake to appreciate it. On the other hand he could at least rest assured that Reality, with its smooth and rough edges, would never bother him again.

The Tarot Moon is another warning for Endymion. If you escape into fantasy, my rosy-cheeked lover, you may never be able to return, and yet the world will always spin on without you.

And the message is for Ruth, too. The next card in the Arcana is the Sun. Can you reach it? Or will you stay for ever in the shadow of the Moon, Ruari pressing you down into darkness, being loved only in your sleep, whilst out there in the real world your flesh daughter is even now battling for her life?

Behind those flickering dreaming eyes a hand is being dealt, but Fortune is not yet ready to reveal herself.

Julie is barely conscious now. Behind her, in the distance, the Mimi has become a ghost-ship as she drifts slowly above the depths, the limp cargo roped to her bows still visible in the mist.

The sea is trying to seduce Julie, trying to suck her down below the waves, but she ignores it.

Instead she watches her mother.

Ruth is laughing at the spray flying in her face. She flings a plump arm around the girl beside her and they both scream with delight as the boat flies across the waves.

They cling to each other with briny wet hands, and when their eyes meet they sparkle like the sea.

Julie leans against her mother to soak in the warmth of her body and breathes in perfumes of salt and tobacco and chocolate.

I really love her, she thinks, surprised, I really do.

When Ruth opens her mouth wide to catch even more of the spray, she motions to Julie to do the same, and together they try to swallow the ocean dry...

...then Julie realises she's stopped fighting. Exhausted, she has surrendered to the embrace of the waves and instead of resisting the water she is gulping it down, trying to hasten the end.

She just wants to rest, to sleep... and then suddenly she hears the

155

lonely cry of a seagull.

By now her tissues are sodden and swollen, her eyes so puffed that she is blinded by her own flesh, but she hears the bird and her vitality is renewed.

Then another bird calls, and she knows she cannot be far from land now, although she can see nothing but a painful slit of light.

She starts to kick once more but soon afterwards she is abruptly caught in a roaring torrent which crashes against her aching ribs, and she almost gives up for the last time.

But the hardness is not the sea — she is being thrown against a cluster of sharp rocks and beneath her bare feet she can feel the pull of shingle.

For a moment she manages to stand upright on her shaky legs before falling again as the water swills around her waist. Pulling herself along like a seal she reaches a line of sharp dry seaweed and collapses onto the sand.

It is nearly dawn.

She has drifted in the coastal currents for twelve hours, to be finally washed up on the beach of a small private hotel.

The grumpy gardener mumbles his way across the sand to gather kelp for his vegetable beds and finds instead a disfigured mermaid sleeping in the autumn sun.

An hour later the Mimi rattles into the shallows of a nearby bay.

She is trailing a lesser Captain Ahab, his toes dragging in the shingle, his cut-price binoculars still around his neck. It's obvious that he's suffered the common fate of those who challenge the sea. These amateur sailors...

As the sun lifts away the blue veil of night it scoops up the enveloping Ruari from his lover's sleeping form and carries him high above the drying land until he is no more than the cloud of moisture in an exhaled breath.

Making a last sad farewell to Ruth — a single tear on her cheek — he yields to the warm and airy solar caresses and awaits his next delicious transmutation.

It is a new day.

There is a wooden bench along the south wall of the house, and

156

beside it an old round wrought-iron table, painted white. Honeysuckle reaches down from a mass of trellis work and fingertips Ruth's curly hair as she sits in the sun.

Beside her are a tray of coffee and some ginger biscuits. She has a pad on her knee, and she is writing a list. Wood, screws, nails, and wire. She uses a fountain pen newly-filled with green ink.

There won't be many more mornings like this before the winter sets in, but with luck the weather will hold long enough for building.

Meanwhile, the hens must be kept warm and dry.

Nothing can be done about the ruined shed they used to live in. It has already floated far downstream, so for the moment Ruth has resigned herself to their wandering amongst the vegetables. Most of the leeks and cabbages have been washed away anyway.

This afternoon she will clear an area of the garage and build temporary nest-boxes and a roost, so that the hens have somewhere to call their own until their new house is built. It will take at least a week before the structure will be ready.

Closing her eyes, Ruth puts down her pen and leans against the honeysuckle. The sun breathes gently on her lids and caresses her warm skin.

She is content.

She had woken that morning with the strange yet comfortable feeling of having dozed for only a few minutes, although in fact she had slept soundly for nearly ten hours. Yet she sprang from unremembered dreams into a state of full wakefulness and with an urgent feeling that it was time to be up and doing.

She hesitated only just long enough to enjoy the caress of the cool smooth sheets along her legs before throwing them off, leaping to her feet, and walking over to the window. Her limbs felt supple and well-exercised, her joints fluid in their movements.

Julie was drowning in hospital pillows.

She dreamed of her mother's face peering down through the ice, her features obscured by clouds of steam as she gently poured a kettle to and fro across the surface.

The ice stretched and shifted, but it would not melt.

157

As if nothing had ever happened, the river flowed innocently along its accustomed path. It was perhaps dirtier than usual, and still floating with assorted wreckage, but at least it had slowed and shrunk to normal size.

Its banks, however, were slippery muddy scars embedded with furniture and broken trees. Hundreds of metres on either side showed slimy evidence that nature had once again asserted itself upon the landscape.

Now it was making amends. A clear and cloudless sky distributed winter sunshine evenly over the earth, soothing and consoling with benevolence.

At her bedroom window, Ruth pulled the yellow shirt away from the sill and stretched out an arm to catch the rays of heat. She smiled, sensing the muscles pulling her lips and cheeks into an unaccustomed shape. Her eyes felt washed and clean, and wider than before.

She realised it had been a long time.

Then her attention was caught by a subdued flashing inside the room. The digital bedside alarm was winking, telling her that the electricity was back on and time was waiting to be re-started.

She looked around the room.

Ruari was missing.

Not even the scent of him remained, but his absence seemed to make a wider space, and she suddenly realised that there were areas of this house she had never properly seen before.

Chilled to the bone, Julien could barely breath.

She finned listlessly back and forth in the dark.
Too cold, too tired, to try any more.

Exhausted, she sensed a distant numbing pain as her scales scraped harshly against the side of the pool.

The clock was also a radio.

'...after yesterday's widespread flooding in The Midlands, all major roads are now passable with care. For more detailed information, please tune to your local radio station.

158

'And now the time is seven o'clock on this Sunday morning, December the...'

Ruth pressed the buttons and set the digital clock. So it was seven a.m. All across the country everyone agreed that it was seven a.m. Well, a reasonable hour to begin living by.

Real time. No dispute.

Then she realised that if there was electricity, there might also be fresh water. In the bathroom she tried the cold tap and found it working, so she pulled the shower cord and climbed in.

This was her luxury. Instantaneous and electric, it massaged her with fine needles of hot spray. She washed her hair vigorously then closed her eyes and turned her face into the deluge. The steaming water scrubbed at her skin as she stood hypnotised by sensation, flicking the dial to Cold, then back again to Hot, until her whole body felt invigorated and pinkly fresh.

She rubbed herself dry and chose some warm clothes from the airing cupboard. A navy t-shirt; a smooth lambswool sweater, also dark blue, and scented with traces of her own perfume, and pale work-softened jeans.

Then she turned off the radio and went downstairs to be greeted rapturously by Sophie.

Ruth filled the automatic kettle, switched it on, and went out to join the hens in the sunshine.

The air was marsh-mallow light on the birds' feathers. Their red combs flopped from side to side as they snipped at unwary woodlice around the door-step and Ruth stood watching them with pleasure until the kettle clicked and she went back inside to prepare a tray of fresh coffee.

Amongst the cushions of the sitting-room sofa she found three big brown speckled eggs which she collected up and nursed delicately against her cheek.

Now she takes a ginger biscuit and bites. It fizzes spicy on her tongue, then melts. She sips the hot coffee and offers a morsel of biscuit to the dog.

It's eight a.m. They have the whole day before them.

The first day.

A sudden twist in her stomach reminds her of the prospect of life without Ruari, but she quells it. There is a sadness at his going, but from somewhere she has found the desire to live in the world without him and it finally feels like peace.

159

At last the ice is cracking, and her mother leans over to plunge an arm into the glassy water. Julie feels herself grasped by a firm hand and pulled into the bitter air.

For a moment she is unable to breathe, her gasping body filled with terror at the unfamiliar emptiness of the world beyond the pool. Then suddenly her lungs fill and she finds that she can cry out.

Immediately a nearby patient comes hurrying to lean over her with a smile which is not Ruth's.

She avoids the greeting and turns her gaze instead towards the round pale lights in the ceiling. They remind her of something — hot coins against a frosty window. Steaming kettles boiling a crater in an icy pond.

Now she can remember the water. But it's not a memory of Beaufort's Dyke, nor of her salt-rinsed fingers, nor of a glugging drowning traitor — but a recollection felt only against her cool cheeks — a remembrance of light spray flying across the bows of a fast boat, and waves leaping into her hair.

And the warm smell of wet skin...

Peace at last.

Yesterday Ruth's emotions had been in full flood with the river. There was no design to it, but it was true that over the years the natural slope of her life had been steepening into a rapid descent. Which, for the most part, she had truthfully indulged. She had deliberately hidden herself away in the house well above the high-water mark. It was easier to take an imaginary lover than to confront a real relationship, and Ruari had become so much part of her life that she often forgot his ephemerality.

She'd been lonely for so long.

But today the morning passes by in a haze of sunshine and work.

Fortunately the house has remained dry, and it does not take long to clean up the sitting-room, wipe away the muddy footprints, and remake the fire. She is interrupted only by the need to shoo away the hens who now see no reason why they should not return to their cosy roost on the sofa. But that was only tolerated in a time of emergency. Now, Ruth wants everything ship-shape.

At noon she returns to her bench to rest and reflect.

She is proud of herself. She has achieved all this on her own, hardly noticing Ruari's absence. She feels freer, lighter, than ever before.

Powerful.

For the first time in a long time she allows herself to wonder what Julie is doing at this very moment. She picks up the phone to call her, but the line's still dead. Maybe later...

The ward is busy today, and they are happy to discharge Julie if she feels well enough to leave. Simon's body is in the mortuary. The policeman, busily filling in forms, offers his condolences.

After a hospital lunch she takes a taxi back to Simon's house, extracts a key from the plastic bag of his belongings, and unlocks the door.

It's strange. With Simon's death the place has immediately lost all memory of him. Shocked by this rush of emptiness she stumbles and leans against the door for support. But as soon as she closes her eyes he opens his to survey her with the vacant gaze of the recently drowned.

She stares back at him, unmoved.

You asked for it, she says aloud.

She cannot wait to get out of there. Picking up her case from the hallway, she leaves the house to its chill reverie and, with equal finality, locks the door behind her. The silver car is still parked outside, ready and waiting to go.

Ruth is in the garage hammering the last nest-box into place when she reaches for a cigarette only to find that she has smoked them all. A wave of panic pushes through her veins, but she quells

161

it. Maybe this is a good time to stop, for once and for ever. There have been too many addictions in her life but today she feels strong enough to join battle. She flexes her empty fingers and senses the cool dry air between them. It feels good.

Shading her eyes from the warm gaze of the evening sun, she scans the view to find a tiny silver dot winding its way along the muddy road by the river. It passes the house downstream, the pale blue caravan now snuggled against its grimy walls, then turns left and begins the short ascent up the hill.

Julie is almost home.

Meanwhile, it is noon somewhere else in the world where a woman lies sunbathing beside a rippling swimming pool. Behind closed lids, she is dreaming of a lover.

She does not know that even as his face grows in her mind he is collecting like dew in the rivulets of sweat beneath her breasts, and in her sleep she shivers at the damp touch of fingers as light as breath.

Sensing her desire, the sun has brought her a gift from across the world and already there is the sudden wet taste of salt upon her lips.